John Ford's The Lover's Melancholy: A Retelling

David Bruce

Published by David Bruce, 2022.

JOHN FORD'S THE LOVER'S MELANCHOLY: A RETELLING

First edition. July 9, 2022.

Copyright © 2022 David Bruce.

ISBN: 979-8201058272

Written by David Bruce.

Table of Contents

Dedication

Dedicated to My Uncle Reuben Saturday

When he was a young man, my mother's brother Reuben wanted to escape from poverty and lard sandwiches, so he tried to run away from it. He stole a car so he could drive up north where he hoped to find opportunity, but he got caught and ended up on a Georgia chain gang for several months. In a chain gang, prisoners are shackled every few feet by the ankles to a long length of chain to keep them from escaping. They work in the hot sun while shackled to the chain, and when they sleep, they are shackled to the bed. No freedom, hard work, hot sun, no pay, bad food, and some mean guards.

When my uncle got released from the chain gang, he hitchhiked up north. He did what a lot of people trying to escape from poverty do: He drifted. He drifted from town to town, seeking opportunity and not finding it. He worked when he could, but the jobs were temporary and low pay. My uncle slept rough often, and he was hungry often. Once, when he was completely broke and completely hungry, he saw a restaurant with a buffet and went inside and asked to speak to the manager. He said, "I am very hungry, I don't have any money, and I would appreciate it very much if you would give me any food that the restaurant is going to throw away. I will be happy to wait by the rear entrance until you are ready to throw away food."

The manager told him to sit down at a table, and then the manager went to the buffet, loaded a big plate high with food, and gave it to him free of charge.

One way out of poverty is to get a good job, and my uncle got out of poverty by getting a job working with sheet metal.

My uncle's work ethic helped him. His employer sent him to California to do some special sheet-metal work, and the people in California wanted to keep him there. They explained that their California employees liked to come to work late, leave early, and take many days off. It was difficult to get someone who would show up and do the work they were supposed to do and were paid to do.

My uncle was also good with money. He got married, bought a house, and raised six children. Each time he made a mortgage payment, he paid extra money so he could pay off the mortgage faster.

If there was a sale on food, he bought lots of it. For example, if there was a sale on peanut butter, two jars for the price of one, he would buy twelve jars and sometimes go back the next day and buy six more jars.

If you went in his pantry — a closet set aside to store food — you saw that it was packed with food. If you went in his kitchen, you saw that he had taken off the doors of the high cabinets in which he stored food so that he could see the food. If you went in his bedroom, you saw that he had all the regular bedroom furniture, but he also had lots of shelves he had installed. The shelves were loaded with things that he had bought on sale that he knew his family could use: food (of course), light bulbs, toothpaste, toilet paper, etc. His bedroom looked like a warehouse.

Once he made a bad purchase: he bought a case of baked beans. Beans are beans, but the sauce they came in can taste good or bad, and the sauce these beans came in tasted bad. His kids told him, "Dad, throw those beans away! They're awful!"

But when you grow up poor, you don't throw beans away. For a long time, whenever my uncle and his family ate baked beans, they ate a mixture of one can of good baked beans and one can of bad baked beans.

My uncle's kids never had to eat lard sandwiches.

***

The doing of good deeds is important. As a free person, you can choose to live your life as a good person or as a bad person. To be a good person, do good deeds. To be a bad person, do bad deeds. If you do good deeds, you will become good. If you do bad deeds, you will become bad. To become the person you want to be, act as if you already are that kind of person. Each of us chooses what kind of person we will become. To become a good person, do the things a good person does. To become a bad person, do the things a bad person does. The opportunity to take action to become the kind of person you want to be is yours.

Cover Photograph for John Ford's *The Lover's Melancholy*: A Retelling:

Image by StockSnap from Pixabay.

Educate Yourself
Read Like A Wolf Eats
Be Excellent to Each Other
Books Then, Books Now, Books Forever

***

In this retelling, as in all my retellings, I have tried to make the work of literature accessible to modern readers who may lack the knowledge about mythology, religion, and history that the literary work's contemporary audience had.

Do you know a language other than English? If you do, I give you permission to translate this book, copyright your translation, publish or self-publish it, and keep all the royalties for yourself. (Do give me credit, of course, for the original retelling.)

I would like to see my retellings of classic literature used in schools, so I give permission to the country of Finland (and all other countries) to give copies of this book to all students forever. I also give permission to the state of Texas (and all other states) to give copies of this book to all students forever. I also give permission to all teachers to give copies of this book to all students forever.

Teachers need not actually teach my retellings. Teachers are welcome to give students copies of my eBooks as background material. For example, if they are teaching Homer's *Iliad* and *Odyssey*, teachers are welcome to give students copies of my *Virgil's* Aeneid: *A Retelling in Prose* and tell students, "Here's another ancient epic you may want to read in your spare time."

CAST OF CHARACTERS

Male Characters

PALADOR, prince of Cyprus. His late father was named Agenor.

AMETHUS, cousin to Prince Palador.

MELEANDER, an old lord. Formerly a statesman to Prince Palador's father.

SOPHRONOS, brother to Meleander, and counselor to Prince Palador.

MENAPHON, son of Sophronos.

PARTHENOPHILL, companion to Menaphon; young, good-looking, and talented.

ARETUS, tutor to Prince Palador.

CORAX, a physician.

RHETIAS, a reduced-in-status courtier.

PELIAS, a foolish courtier.

CUCULUS, a foolish courtier.

TROLLIO, servant to Meleander.

Female Characters

THAMASTA, sister of Amethus, and cousin to the Prince.

EROCLEA, daughter of Meleander. Has been missing from Cyprus for two years.

CLEOPHILA, daughter of Meleander.

KALA, waiting-maid to Thamasta.

GRILLA, a page of Cuculus. A boy, but wearing women's clothing. This book will refer to Grilla as a "she," rather than a "he."

Other Characters

Officers, Attendants, etc.

***

SCENE

The city of Famagosta on the island of Cyprus.

***

NOTA BENE

In the Prologue, John Ford says that he is not plagiarizing. He does this because his play shows that Richard Burton's *Anatomy of Melancholy* influenced him. Such influence is allowed to scholars, he states, and such influence can delight audiences.

The word "parthenophilia" did not appear in the online *Oxford English Dictionary* as of 30 June 2024, but Wiktionary defines it in this way:

"Noun. Parthenophilia (uncountable)

"Sexual attraction towards girls in late adolescence."

https://en.wiktionary.org/wiki/parthenophilia

In this society, the word "wench" is not necessarily negative; it is often used affectionately.

BACKSTORY

These are some elements of the backstory of this play:

• Meleander has two daughters: Eroclea and Cleophila.

• The ruler of Cyprus (Prince Palador's father) wanted Prince Palador to marry Eroclea.

• The ruler of Cyprus (Prince Palador's father) fell in lust with Eroclea when she appeared at his court.

• To protect her virtue, Eroclea disappeared.

• Prince Palador, who loves Eroclea, became and still is melancholic.

• The ruler of Cyprus (Prince Palador's father) accused Meleander of treason and disgraced him.

• As a result of his disgrace, Meleander became mentally ill, and his daughter Cleophila takes care of him.

• The ruler of Cyprus (Prince Palador's father) died, and Prince Palador became the ruler of Cyprus.

• As the play opens, Eroclea has been missing for two years.

• As the play opens, Menaphon (son of Sophronos, who is the brother of Meleander) and Amethus (a cousin of Prince Palador) are also disappointed in love.

• As the play opens, Menaphon loves Thamasta — Amethus' sister — but she does not return his love.

• As the play opens, Amethus loves Cleophila, but she devotes herself to taking care of her father, Meleander.

• As the play opens, Prince Palador loves Eroclea, but she has been missing for two years.

PROLOGUE

To tell you, gentlemen, in what true sense
    The writer, actors, or the audience
    Should mold their judgments for a play, might draw
    Truth into rules; but we have no such law.
    Our writer, for himself, would have you know
    That in his following scenes he does not owe
    To others' fancies, nor has lain in wait
    For any stolen invention, from whose height
    He might commend his own, more than the right
    A scholar claims, may warrant for delight.
    It is art's scorn, that some of late [recently] have made
    The noble use of poetry a trade.
    For your parts, gentlemen, to quit his pains [reward the playwright's efforts],
    Yet you will please, that as you meet with strains
    Of lighter mixture, but to cast your eye
    Rather upon the main [main route] than on the bye [byway],
    His hopes stand firm, and we shall find it true,
    THE LOVER'S MELANCHOLY cured by you.
    Note: Two meanings of the verb "cured" are "healed" and "protected." The audience can protect John Ford's play by applauding it and making it a success.

CHAPTER 1

— 1.1 —

Menaphon and Pelias talked together in a room in the palace. Pelias was a foolish courtier. Menaphon, the son of Sophronos, had just returned from his yearlong travels.

"Dangers!" Menaphon said. "What do you mean by dangers — you who in so courtly fashion congratulate my safe return from dangers?"

"I congratulate your safe return from your travels, noble sir," Pelias said.

"My travels are delights," Menaphon said, "as long as my experience of travel has not, like a truant, misspent the time — time that I have striven to use for bettering my mind with observation."

"As I am modest, I protest it is strange," Pelias said. "But is it possible?"

"Is what possible?" Menaphon asked.

"To bestride the frothy foams of the sea-god Neptune's surging waves, when Boreas the blustering North Wind tosses up the deep and thumps a thunder-bounce?"

"Sweet sir, it is nothing," Menaphon said. "Immediately comes a dolphin, playing near your ship, heaving his crooked back up, and presents you with a metaphorical feather-bed so it can waft you to the shore as easily as if you slept in the court."

According to Pliny's *Natural History* (Book 9, Chapter 8), friendly dolphins allow humans to ride on their backs.

"Indeed!" Pelias said. "Is it true, I ask you?"

"I will not stretch your faith upon the tenters," Menaphon replied.

Tenters are wooden frameworks on which cloth could be stretched for drying.

Menaphon continued, "Please tell me, Pelias, where did you learn this language?"

Pelias had been using inflated, poetic language.

"I this language!" Pelias said. "Alas, sir, we who study words and forms of compliment must fashion all discourse according to the nature of the subject."

Seeing some people coming, Pelias said, "But I am silent. Now appears a sun, whose shadow I adore."

It's an unusual sun that has a shadow.

Amethus, Sophronos, and some attendants entered the room. Amethus was a cousin of Prince Palador of Cyprus. Sophronos was Menaphon's father and an advisor to Prince Palador.

"My honored father!" Menaphon said.

"From my eyes, son, son of my care, my love, the joys that bid you welcome do too much proclaim that I am a child," Sophronos said.

He was weeping like a child.

"Oh, princely sir," Menaphon said to Amethus. "Give me your hand."

Amethus was a close friend who ranked high in Prince Palador's court.

"Perform your duties where you owe them first," Amethus replied.

In other words, respect your father and show attention to him before you show attention to me.

Amethus added, "I dare not interrupt the pleasures your presence has brought home."

Speaking about Amethus, Sophronos said to Menaphon, "Here you find a friend still as noble, Menaphon, as he was when you left at your departure."

"Yes, I know it," Menaphon said. "To him I owe more service —"

Amethus interrupted, "Please excuse me."

He said to Sophronos, "Menaphon shall attend your entertainments soon, the next day, and the next day after that. For an hour or two, I want to monopolize him and be alone with him."

"Noble lord!" Sophronos said, surprised.

Amethus must have something important to talk about with Menaphon. Otherwise, he would not be so abrupt despite his desire not to be abrupt, and he would not monopolize Menaphon despite his desire to let Menaphon greet and respect his father.

Amethus said to Sophronos and Pelias, "You're both dismissed."

"I am your creature and your servant," Pelias said. "I am wholly yours."

Everyone except Amethus and Menaphon exited.

"Give me your hand," Amethus said. "I will not say, 'You are welcome.' That is the common way of common friends. I'm glad I have you here. Oh, I lack the words I need to let you know what is my heart!"

"Your heart is joined to my heart," Menaphon said.

"Yes, it is," Amethus said. "They are joined as firmly as that holy thing called friendship can unite our hearts.

"Menaphon, my Menaphon, may now all the goodly blessings that can create a heaven on earth dwell with you!

"For twelve months we have been separated, but from henceforth we never more will part, until that sad hour in which death leaves one of us behind, to see the other's funeral rites performed.

"Let's now for a while be free and frank and unrestrained.

"How have your travels abroad relieved you of your discontent?"

"Such cure as sick men find in changing beds, I found in change of airs," Menaphon said. "The fancy flattered my hopes with ease, as theirs do, but the grief is still the same."

Menaphon had traveled for a year to escape his melancholy, but despite the promise of relief, he was still melancholic.

"Such is my case at home," Amethus said. "Cleophila, your kinswoman, that maiden of sweetness and humility, pities more her father's poor afflictions than the tide of my lover's complaints."

Cleophila was the daughter of Meleander, who was the brother of Sophronos, who was Menaphon's father. Therefore, Cleophila and Menaphon were first cousins.

Menaphon said, "Thamasta, my great mistress, your princely sister, has, I hope, before this time conferred and confirmed affection on some worthy choice."

Both Amethus and Menaphon were unlucky in love.

Amethus loved Cleophila, but she preferred to look after her ill father.

Menaphon loved Thamasta — the word "mistress" meant "loved one" — but she did not return his love. Menaphon had traveled abroad for a year to recover from his grief at not being loved, but his attempt to cure his grief was unsuccessful.

Amethus replied, "She has not given her affection to anyone, Menaphon. Her bosom still is walled around with ice, although, by the truth of love, no day has ever passed during which I have not mentioned your deserts, your constancy, your — truly, I dare not tell you what, lest you might think I fawned on and flattered you. That is a sin that friendship was never guilty of, for flattery is monstrous in a true friend."

"Does the court wear the old looks, too?" Menaphon asked.

Amethus replied, "If you are referring to Prince Palador, it does. He's the same melancholy man he was at his father's death. Sometimes he speaks sense, but seldom mirth. He will smile, but seldom laugh. He will lend an ear to business, but deal in none. He will gaze upon revels, antic fopperies, and grotesque entertainments, but not be entertained by them. He will sparingly discourse and hear music, but what he takes most delight in are handsome pictures.

"Stories have seldom mentioned one so young and goodly, so sweet in his own nature."

Menaphon said, "It's no wonder that such as I am groan under the light burdens of small sorrows, when a prince so potent as he cannot shun the agitations of passion. To be a man, my lord, is to be but the exercise of cares in several different shapes. As miseries grow, they alter as do men's forms, but how no one knows."

"This little isle of Cyprus surely abounds in greater wonders both for change and fortune than any wonders you have seen abroad," Amethus said.

Menaphon said, "Surely more than any wonders I have observed abroad. All countries on any other supposition than change and fortune yield something rare to a free eye and mind, and I, for my part, have brought home one jewel of admirable value."

"A jewel, Menaphon?" Amethus asked.

"A jewel, my Amethus," Menaphon said. "This jewel is a fair youth — a youth, whom, if I were superstitious, I should consider to have an excellence higher than mere creations are."

To Menaphon, this fair youth seemed to be more an immortal god than a mortal creature — that is, if Menaphon were superstitious and believed in supernatural beings.

Menaphon continued, "To add delight, I'll tell you how I found him."

"Please, do," Amethus said.

"Passing from Italy to Greece, the tales that poets of an elder time have created to glorify their Tempe, a valley between Mount Olympus and Mount Ossa in Thessaly, bred in me the desire of visiting that paradise," Menaphon said. "To Thessaly I came, and living privately, without the acquaintance of sweeter companions than the old inmates to my love — I refer to my thoughts — I day by day frequented silent groves and solitary walks.

"One early morning I encountered this incident: I heard the sweetest and most ravishing contention that art and nature ever were at strife in."

"I cannot yet conceive what you mean by art and nature," Amethus said.

Menaphon said, "I shall soon explain that.

"A sound of music touched my ears, or rather indeed entranced my soul. As I stole nearer, invited by the melody, I saw this youth, this fair-faced youth, upon his lute, with strains of strange variety and harmony, proclaiming, as it seemed, so bold a challenge to the clear choristers of the woods, the birds, that, as they flocked about him, all stood silent, marveling at what they heard. I marveled, too."

"And so do I, good man!" Amethus said. "Go on!"

Menaphon said, "A nightingale, nature's best-skilled musician, undertook the challenge, and for all the different strains of melody the well-shaped youth could touch, she sang her chorus.

"The youth could not play rapid melodic passages with more art upon his quaking instrument than she, the nightingale, replied to with her various notes.

"For a voice and for a sound, Amethus, it is much easier to believe that such they were than hope to hear again."

"How did the rivals part?" Amethus asked.

Menaphon said, "You term them rightly, for they were rivals, and their mistress, harmony.

"Some time thus spent, the young man grew at last into a pretty anger because a bird, whom art had never taught musical clefts, moods, or notes, would vie for mastery with him, who had busily spent many hours devoted to study and perfect practice.

"To end the controversy, in a rapture upon his instrument the young man played so swiftly, with so many spontaneous passages, and so lively, that there were ingenuity and skill, concord in discord, and lines of differing method meeting in one full concentration of delight."

"Now for the bird," Amethus said.

Menaphon said, "The bird, ordained to be music's first martyr, strove to imitate these several different sounds, which when her warbling throat failed in, out of grief the nightingale dropped down on his lute, and broke her heart.

"It was the quaintest sadness to see the conqueror weep a funeral elegy of tears upon the nightingale's resting place.

"Trust me, my Amethus, I could chide my own unmanly weakness that made me a fellow-mourner with him."

Menaphon had also wept.

"I believe you," Amethus said.

Menaphon said, "He looked upon the trophies of his art, then sighed, then wiped his eyes, then sighed and cried, 'Alas, poor creature! I will soon revenge this cruelty upon the author of it. Henceforth this lute, guilty of innocent blood, shall never more betray a harmless peace to a premature end,' and in that sorrow, as he was bashing his lute against a tree, I suddenly stepped in."

"You have discoursed a true tale of entertainment and pity," Amethus said.

Menaphon said, "I reprieved the intended execution with entreaties and interruption.

"But, my princely friend, it was not strange that the music of his hand overmatched the birds, when his voice and beauty, youth, carriage, and discretion must, from men endowed with reason, ravish admiration.

"From me they did."

"But is this miracle not to be seen?" Amethus asked.

Menaphon said, "I persuaded him by degrees to choose me to be his companion. From where he comes, or who he is, as I dared to modestly inquire, so gently he would plead not to make known only for reasons to himself reserved.

"He told me that some remnant of his life was to be spent in travel. As for his fortunes, they were neither mean nor riotous, neither poor nor wealthy enough to engage in riotous living. His friends were not famous in the world, although they were not obscure.

"His country is Athens, and his name is Parthenophill."

"Did he come with you to Cyprus?" Amethus asked.

"Willingly," Menaphon said. "The fame of our young melancholy prince, Meleander's strange mental disturbances, the obedience of young Cleophila,

Thamasta's glory, your matchless friendship, and my desperate love, prevailed with him; and I have lodged him privately in the city of Famagosta."

"Now you are doubly welcome," Amethus said. "You and your guest are both welcome. I will not lose the sight of such a rarity for one part of my hopes — I will be able to enjoy the companionship of both yourself and this splendid youth.

"When do you intend to visit my great-spirited sister?"

"May I visit her without causing offence?" Menaphon asked.

"Yes, without offence," Amethus said. "Parthenophill shall also find worthy entertainment during the visit.

"You are not still a coward? You will visit her?"

"She's too excellent, and I'm too low in merit," Menaphon said.

"I'll prepare a noble welcome," Amethus said, "and, friend, before we part, I will unload to you an overcharged heart."

They exited.

— 1.2 —

Rhetias, a reduced-in-status courtier who was carelessly dressed, stood alone in another room in the palace. He was so reduced in status that foolish courtiers such as Pelias called him "sirrah," a term that a man of higher status called a man of lower status.

He had been abroad but had just returned to Cyprus.

Rhetias was cynical and seriously thought about Stoic ideas.

He said to himself, "I will not court the madness of the times, nor fawn upon the riots that embalm our wanton gentry, to preserve the dust of their affected vanities in coffins of memorable shame.

"When commonwealths totter and reel from that nobility and ancient virtue that make renowned the great, who steer the helm of government, while mushrooms grow up, and make new laws to license folly, why shouldn't I, a May-game — a laughing-stock — scorn the weight of my sunken fortunes?"

He was saying that times were bad, and mushrooms — upstarts quickly gaining prominence in politics — were springing up and passing laws that permitted foolish behavior.

Rhetias continued, "Why shouldn't I snarl at the vices that rot the land, and, without fear of consequences or use of discretion, be my own buffoon?

"It is an entertainment to live when life is irksome, if we will not value prosperity in others and if we will not condemn affliction in ourselves.

"This rule is certain: He who seeks his safety and security from the study of statecraft must learn to be a madman or a fool.

"Ambition, wealth, ease, I renounce the devil that damns you here on earth.

"Either I will be my own source of amusement, or my own tormentor. So be it!"

He could either laugh at his misfortune or wallow in his despair.

Seeing Pelias the foolish courtier coming toward him, he said to himself, "Here comes news — gossip about the court."

Pelias said, "Rhetias, I have sought you out to tell you news — new, excellent new news.

"Cuculus, sirrah, that gull, that young old gull, is coming this way."

A gull is a simpleton.

Cuculus, like Pelias, was a foolish courtier.

Rhetias asked, "And you are his forerunner?"

Great men had heralds who were called forerunners. Cuculus was not a great man, nor was Pelias.

"Please, listen to me," Pelias said. "Instead of a page dressed in the finely trimmed livery of a servant, we've got him a boy, whom we tricked out in neat and handsome fashion.

"We have persuaded Cuculus that the boy is indeed a wench, and he has hired him.

"The boy follows Cuculus, carries his sword and shield, waits on him as he eats, fills his cup with wine, and fills his pipe with tobacco. The boy whets Cuculus' knife, attends to his letters, and does whatever other service Cuculus would employ his manservant in.

"Of course, it is irregular to hire a wench instead of a manservant to do these things.

"Being asked why he is so irregular in courtly etiquette, Cuculus' answer is that since great ladies use gentlemen-ushers to go bare-headed before them as a sign of respect, he knows no reason why he may not reduce the courtiers to have women wait on them, and he begins the fashion.

"Cuculus is laughed at most courteously, and you will burst out laughing when you see him."

Rhetias said, "Agelastus, so surnamed for his gravity, was a very wise fellow and kept his countenance all the days of his life as demurely as a judge who pronounces the sentence of death on a poor rogue for stealing as much bacon as would serve at a meal with a calf's head. Yet he smiled once, and never but once. Are you no scholar?"

Agelastus is a nickname that means "unsmiling." This nickname was given to Marcus Crassus, who was the grandfather of the very wealthy Marcus Licinius Crassus, a triumvir in the First Triumvirate, consisting of Julius Caesar, Pompey, and Crassus.

"I have read pamphlets dedicated to me," Pelias said. "Do you call him Agelastus? Why did he laugh?"

'He saw an ass eating thistles," Rhetias replied.

The fable of the ass and thistle is that an ass, heavily loaded with rich foods, stopped to eat a thistle. One interpretation is that one ought not to be a miser and eat poor food when one can afford rich food. In one version of the fable, however, the ass explains that the thistle tastes much better to it than would the rich food, which was for humans.

To laugh at the ass instead of understanding the moral of the fable is to act foolishly. Fooling a fool by dressing a boy in girl's clothing and convincing the fool that the boy is a girl is another example of acting foolishly.

Rhetias continued, "Puppy, go study to be a singular coxcomb. Cuculus is an ordinary ape; but you are an ape of an ape."

For an adult human to be called a puppy, coxcomb (fool), or ape is an insult.

Apes mimic humans, but they are not human.

Pelias said, "You have letters patent to abuse your friends."

Rhetias was not a licensed Fool who had permission to be cutting in remarks even to those socially above him, but his reputation for cutting remarks was widely known and tolerated.

Pelias said, "Look, look, Cuculus is coming! Observe him seriously."

Cuculus walked over to them. His new servant Grilla, a boy who was dressed as a girl, followed him.

Cuculus ordered Grilla, "Give me my sword and buckler."

"Here they are, indeed," Grilla said, handing him the items.

"What is this now, minx? What is this?" Cuculus said, upset by Grilla's lack of courtesy.

He asked, "Where is your duty, your distance? Let me have service methodically tendered; you are now one of us. Give me your curtsy."

Grilla curtsied like a girl.

Cuculus said, "Good! Remember that you are to practice courtly etiquette. Was your father a piper, did you say?"

"He was a sounder of some such wind instrument, indeed," Grilla replied.

The wind instrument could have been his anus, if he were inclined to flatulence. Or he may have been a sow-gelder who blew a horn to announce his presence and availability to work.

"Was he so?" Cuculus said. "Hold up your head. Be you musical to me, and I will marry you to a dancer, one prosperous enough who shall ride on a horse with a footcloth, and I will maintain you in your muff and hood."

At this time, muffs were still fashionable at court, but hoods were not.

"That will be fine indeed," Grilla said.

"You are still just simple," Cuculus said.

"Do you think so?" Grilla asked.

"I have a brain, I have a head-piece — a skull," Cuculus said. "On my conscience, if I were to take pains to work with you, I would raise your understanding, girl, to the height of a nurse, or a court-midwife at least. I will make you big in time, wench."

He was saying that he could work with her and increase her intelligence, but the words he used had bawdy meanings.

A penis raises itself and stands up. A woman in the missionary position understands — is under the stand of a man. To be made big can mean 1) to rise in society, or 2) to become pregnant.

"Even do your pleasure with me, sir," Grilla said. "Do what you want with me."

"Noble, accomplished Cuculus!" Pelias said.

"Give me your fist, innocent," Rhetias said.

One meaning of "fist" is hand.

An innocent is a simpleton, a natural fool with a low IQ.

"I wish it were in your belly!" Cuculus said.

Rhetias had a reputation for being insulting, and Cuculus was insulting him: Cuculus was saying that he would like to use his fist to hit Rhetias in the belly. The insult, however, was in the nature of joking between friends and so Cuculus held out his hand and said, "There it is."

They shook hands.

"That's well," Pelias said. "Rhetias is an honest blade, although he can be blunt."

An honest blade is a good fellow.

Pelias was punning on "blunt blade": 1) a dull sword, and 2) an outspoken fellow.

"Who cares?" Cuculus said. "We can be as blunt as he, for his life."

Rhetias said, "Cuculus, there is, within a mile or two of here, a sow-pig that sucked the milk of a bitch-hound, and now the sow-pig hunts the deer, the hare, and most unnaturally, the wild boar, as well as any hound hunts in Cyprus."

"Monstrous sow-pig!" Cuculus said. "Is it true?"

Pelias said to Rhetias, "I'll host a banquet for you if I can get a sight of the sow-pig."

Rhetias said, "Everything takes after the dam that gave it suck. That is why the sow-pig hunts deer and other meat.

"Where did you get your milk?"

"I?" Cuculus said. "Why, my wet nurse's husband was a most excellent maker of shuttlecocks."

A wet nurse is a woman who suckles another's woman's baby.

Shuttlecocks are made of cork and feathers and are used in such games as badminton.

Pelias said, "My wet nurse was a woman-surgeon."

"And who gave you the pap so you could suck milk, mouse?" Rhetias asked young Grilla.

"I never sucked, that I remember," Grilla said.

Rhetias said, "A shuttlecock-maker! All your brains are stuck with cork and feather, Cuculus.

"This learned courtier — Pelias — takes after the wet nurse, too: a she-surgeon, who is, in effect, a mere matcher of colors."

According to Rhetias, a she-surgeon was a fixer-upper of women's appearances; in other words, a cosmetologist who worked with paint, aka makeup, to bring order out of chaos.

He added, "Go learn to paint and daub compliments — it is the next step to being gifted with a new suit of clothing.

"My Lady Periwinkle here has never sucked. Suck your master, and bring forth mooncalves, fop, do!"

Mooncalves are born fools, unstable people, or monsters. A fop is a fool.

Rhetias added, "This is good philosophy, sirs; make use of it."

"Bless us, what a strange creature this is!" Grilla said.

"He is a gull, an arrant gull by his own proclamation," Cuculus said.

In other words, Rhetias' own words proclaimed him to be a fool.

Corax walked toward them and then began to walk past them.

"Corax, the prince's chief physician!" Pelias said. "What business speeds his haste?"

He then asked Corax, "Are all things well, sir?"

"Yes, yes, yes," Corax answered.

"Phew!" Rhetias said. "You may wheel about and talk to us, man; we know you're proud of your slovenliness and practice; it is your virtue."

"Practice" meant 1) medical practice, and 2) trickery.

Rhetias added, "The prince's melancholy fit, I presume, still continues."

"So do your knavery and desperate beggary," Corax replied.

"Aha!" Cuculus said. "Here's one who will tickle the ban-dog."

A ban-dog is a dog that is tied up because it bites.

"You must not go yet," Rhetias said.

"I'll stay in spite of your teeth," Corax said.

He threw his doctor's gown on the floor and said, "There lies my gravity and seriousness."

He added, "Do whatever you dare to do; I'll withstand you."

He was ready to fight.

Rhetias said, "Mountebanks, empirics, quack-salvers, mineralists, wizards, alchemists, cast-aside apothecaries, old wives and barbers, are all suppositors to the right worshipful doctor, as I take it."

Suppositors are 1) supporters, and 2) suppositories.

Mountebanks sold quack medicines. Empirics were medical quacks who practiced folk medicine. Mineralists advocated the use of minerals in medical practice. Barbers cut hair and also engaged in bloodletting as a form of medical treatment.

Rhetias continued, "Some of you doctors are the head of your art, and the horns, too, but they come by nature. You live as a single man for no other reason but that you fear to be a cuckold."

Cuckolds — men with unfaithful wives — were said to have invisible horns growing out of their heads.

Corax said, "Have at you! Let's fight!

"You practice railing only for your health; your miseries are so thick and so lasting that you haven't even one poor coin to bestow on opening a vein for medical bloodletting. For that reason, in order to avoid a pleurisy, you shall be sure to prate thyself once a month into a whipping, and bleed in the hind parts instead of the arm."

"I say, 'Have at you again!'" Rhetias said. "Let's fight!"

"Come on!" Corax said.

Trying to make peace between the two men, Cuculus said, "There, there, there! Oh, brave doctor!"

Wanting to see them fight, Pelias said, "Let them alone."

Rhetias insulted Corax, "You are in your religion an atheist, in your condition a cur, in your diet an epicure, in your lust a goat, and in your sleep a hog.

"You take upon you the clothing of a grave physician, but you are indeed an impostorous empiric. Physicians are the cobblers — or, rather, the botchers — of men's bodies.

"As the one patches our tattered clothes, so the other solders our diseased flesh."

To solder a wound is to close it so that it can heal. This is a hardly a bad thing. A botcher is 1) an incompetent, 2) a mender of clothing.

This "fight" could very well be an act put on by two friends as a form of entertainment for themselves and others. Sometimes, friends insult each other.

Rhetias continued, "Come on! Let's fight!"

Cuculus shouted, "Go to it! Go to it! Hold him to it! Hold him to it! Go to it! Go to it! Go to it!"

Corax insulted Rhetias, "The best worth in you is the corruption of your mind, for that alone entitles you to the dignity of a louse, a thing bred out of the filth and superfluity of ill humors."

In other words, lice breed in corruption — decaying bodies. Rhetias' insults breed in the corruption of his mind. Therefore, Rhetias has the dignity of a louse, which is the best thing about him.

"You bite anywhere, and you bite any man who doesn't defend himself with the clean linen of secure honesty; you dare not come near any man who defends himself with the clean linen of secure honesty."

Corax may want to rethink that insult. Rhetias apparently dares to "bite" Corax, and according to Corax' insult, Rhetias dares not come near any man who defends himself with the clean linen of secure honesty.

Corax continued insulting Rhetias, "You are fortune's idiot, virtue's bankrupt, time's dunghill, manhood's scandal, and your own scourge. You would hang thyself, so wretchedly miserable you are, except that no man will trust you with as much money as will buy a halter with which you can hang yourself, and all your stock to be sold is not worth half as much as may procure a halter for you."

"Ha, ha, ha!" Rhetias said. "This is flattery, gross flattery."

"I have employment for you, and for you all," Corax said. "Tut, these words of ours are but 'good mornings' between us."

In other words, this was a play-fight.

"Are your bottles full?" Rhetias asked.

He was referring to bottles used to collect specimens of urine.

"They are full of rich wine," Corax said. "Let's all suck the bottles together."

"Like so many swine in a trough," Rhetias said.

"I'll train you all for a performance before the prince," Corax said. "We'll see whether that can move him."

"He shall fret or laugh," Rhetias said.

"Must I be one of those in the performance?" Cuculus asked.

"Yes, and your feminine page, too," Corax answered.

"Thanks, most egregiously," Grilla said.

"I will not slack my part," Pelias said.

"Wench, take my shield," Cuculus said.

"All of you come into my chamber," Corax said. "The project is planned and cast; we must pay attention only to time."

Punning on the musical term "time," Rhetias said, "The melody must agree well and yield entertainment when such as these are, knaves and fools, consort."

Amethus and Thamasta, his sister, talked together in a room in Thamasta's house. Kala, Thamasta's waiting-maid, was present.

"Does this look good?" Amethus asked.

"What do you want me to do?" Thamasta asked.

"I don't want you to be like a nouveau riche modishly dressed lady who is newly crept out of the shell of sluttish sweat, and labor into the glittering pomp of ease and wantonness, embroideries, and all these grotesque fashions that make a woman monstrous. I also don't want you to transform your education and a noble birth into contempt and laughter. Sister, sister, she who derives her blood from princes ought to glorify her greatness by humility."

"Then you conclude that I am proud?" Thamasta asked.

"Young Menaphon, my worthy friend, has loved you long and truly," Amethus said. "To witness his obedience to your scorn, this wronged gentleman undertook a voluntary exile of twelve months.

"Why, then, sister, in this time of his absence, haven't you given your affections to some monarch? Why haven't you sent ambassadors to some neighboring king with fawning affirmations of your graces, your rare perfections, and your admirable beauty?

"This would have been a new piece of 'modesty' that would have deserved to be remembered in history!"

Such actions would not have been modest since they involve rejecting Menaphon, who was not a king, in order to pursue a king.

"You're bitter," Thamasta said. "And, brother, by your leave, you are not kindly wise. You are not acting as a brother ought to act. A brother — kin — ought to act more kindly — and kin-ly — toward his sister.

"My freedom is my birth's. I am not bound to fancy those whom you approve, but only those whom I approve.

"Indeed, you are a humble youth! I hear of your visits and your loving commendation to your heart's saint, Cleophila, a virgin of rare excellence. What though she lacks a dowry to maintain a stately greatness?

"Yet it is your gracious sweetness to descend so low; the meekness of your pity leads you!

"She is your dear friend's sister!"

Actually, Cleophila is Amethus' dear friend's — Menaphon's — first cousin.

Thamasta continued, "She is a good soul! An innocent!"

One meaning of "innocent" is "simpleton."

"Thamasta!" Amethus said.

"I have given your Menaphon a welcome home, as befits me," Thamasta said. "For his sake I have entertained Parthenophill, the handsome stranger, more familiarly than, I may fear, becomes me. Yet, for his part, I do not repent my courtesies, but you —"

Amethus interrupted, "No more, no more! Be affable to both. Time may reclaim your cruelty."

Talking about Parthenophill, Thamasta said, "I pity the youth; and, trust me, brother, I love his seriousness. He talks the prettiest stories; he delivers his tales so gracefully that I could sit and listen, and indeed, forget my meals and my sleep, in order to hear his neatly delivered discourses.

"Menaphon was well advised in choosing such a friend to plead his true love."

"Now I commend you," Amethus said. "You shall change at last, I hope."

Thamasta thought, *I fear I shall.*

Menaphon and Parthenophill entered the room.

"Have you seen the garden?" Amethus asked.

"It is an ingenious and pleasantly contrived delight," Menaphon replied.

Thamasta said to Parthenophill, "Your eye, sir, has in your travels often met delights of more variety?"

"No, none, lady," Parthenophill replied.

"It would be impossible, since your fair presence makes every place, where it vouchsafes to shine, more lovely than all other helps of art can equal," Menaphon said to Thamasta.

"What you mean by 'helps of art'?" Thamasta asked. "You know yourself best. Be they as they are. You need none, I am sure, to set me forth and praise me."

"It would be evidence of lack of manners, more than evidence of skill, not to praise praise itself," Menaphon said.

"For your reward, henceforth I'll call you servant," Thamasta said.

By calling Menaphon "servant," Thamasta was recognizing him as her devoted servant — that is, as someone who loved her, and someone who was her wooer.

Pleased, Amethus said, "Excellent sister!"

"It is my first step to honor," Menaphon said. "May I fall lower than shame, when I neglect all service that may confirm this favor! If I neglect you, may I be worse than shamed!"

"Are you well, sir?" Thamasta asked Parthenophill.

"Great princess, I am well," Parthenophill replied. "To see a league between a humble love, such as my friend's is, and a commanding virtue, such as yours is, are sure restoratives."

Thamasta said to Parthenophill, "You speak wittily."

She said to Amethus, "Brother, be pleased to show the gallery to this young stranger. Spend the time a while there, and then we will all go together to the court."

She then said to Parthenophill, "I will present you, sir, to the prince: Palador."

"You are entirely composed of fairness and true bounty," Parthenophill replied.

"Come, come," Amethus said. "We'll await you, sister."

Referring to Thamasta's acceptance of Menaphon as her servant, he said, "This beginning promises future happy events.

"You have blessed me," Menaphon said.

Menaphon, Amethus, and Parthenophill exited, leaving Thamasta and Kala, her serving-maid.

"Kala, oh, Kala!" Thamasta said.

"Lady?" Kala said.

"We share our private thoughts," Thamasta said. "You are metaphorically my cabinet in which I keep secret papers."

"Lock your secrets in a hidden place, then," Kala said. "I am not one to be forced to open up and reveal secrets."

"Never until now could I even think of being a traitor to honor and to modesty," Thamasta said.

"You are in love," Kala said.

"I am grown base," Thamasta said. "Parthenophill!"

She had just criticized her brother for loving someone who lacked wealth; now she had fallen in love with Parthenophill, who lacked wealth.

"He's handsome, richly endowed," Kala said.

Parthenophill was richly endowed with many virtues, but there was no evidence that he was richly endowed with riches.

Kala continued, "He has a lovely face and a winning tongue."

"If ever I must fall, in him my greatness sinks," Thamasta said.

If she were to fall in love with and marry Parthenophill, her social status would fall.

Thamasta continued, "Love is a tyrant, resisted.

"Whisper in his ear and tell him how gladly I would steal time to talk with him one hour. But do it honorably.

"Please, Kala, do not betray me."

"Madam, I will make it my own case," Kala said. "He shall think I am in love with him."

"I hope you are not, Kala," Thamasta said.

"I will say I am for your sake," Kala said. "I'll tell him so; but, truly, I am not in love with him, lady."

"Please, treat me kindly," Thamasta said. "Let me not too soon be lost in my new follies. It is a fate that overrules our wisdoms. While we strive to live most freely, we're caught in our own toils.

"Diamonds cut diamonds; they who will prove to thrive in cunning must cure love with love."

Thamasta was planning to cure Menaphon's love for her by using her love for Parthenophill.

CHAPTER 2

— 2.1 —

Sophronos and Aretus talked together in an apartment in the palace. Sophronos was Prince Palador's counselor, and Aretus was Prince Palador's tutor. A tutor manages the affairs of a person who is incapable of doing so himself. Aretus may also have been Prince Palador's academic tutor. Both Sophronos and Aretus were managing the affairs of Cyprus because Prince Palador was suffering from melancholy.

Sophronos complained, "Our commonwealth is sick. It is more than time that we should wake its head — the prince — who sleeps in the dull lethargy of vanished safety and security.

"The common people murmur, and the nobles grieve. The court is now turned grotesque and grows wild, while all the neighboring nations stand gazing and watch for a suitable opportunity to wreak their justly conceived fury to avenge such injuries as the late prince, our living master's father, committed against laws of truth or honor.

"Intelligence comes flying in on all sides, while the unsteady multitude presume that you, Aretus, and I engross, because of our private ambition, the affairs of government, which I, for my part, groan under and am weary of."

"Sophronos," Aretus said, "I am also as zealous to shake off my gay state-fetters, and so I have thought of a speedy remedy, and to that end, as I have told you, I have been working with Corax, the prince's chief physician."

"You should have done this sooner, Aretus. You were his tutor, and so you could best discern Prince Palador's dispositions in order to shape them rightly."

"Passions of a violent nature are most easily reclaimed by degrees," Aretus said. "There's something hidden that concerns his distemper, which we'll now find out."

Prince Palador was suffering from a mental disturbance, but the reason why was hidden.

Several people entered the room: Corax, Rhetias, Pelias, Cuculus, and Grilla.

Aretus said, "You have come at the exact time for your appointment. Welcome, gentlemen!"

"Have you won over Rhetias, Corax?"

"Most sincerely," Corax said. "He will help."

"May God save you, nobilities!" Cuculus said.

Sophronos and Aretus outranked courtiers such as Cuculus and Pelias.

Cuculus continued, "Do your lordships take notice of my page? It is a fashion of the newest edition, spick and span new, without example."

A page is a personal attendant.

He then ordered Grilla, "Do your honor, housewife."

By "housewife," he meant "girl."

As Grilla curtsied twice, once each to Sophronos and to Aretus, she said, "There's a curtsy for you, and a curtsy for you."

"It is excellent," Sophronos said. "We all must follow fashion, and entertain she-pages."

"It will be courtly," Aretus said.

"I think so," Cuculus said. "I hope the historical chronicles will praise me one day for a headpiece —"

He meant this: I hope the historical chronicles will praise me one day by saying I am an intelligent man, a brain.

"Headpiece," however, had two relevant meanings: 1) brain, or 2) skull (not including the brain).

Using the second meaning, Rhetias interrupted, "— of woodcock, without brains in it!"

Woodcocks were proverbially stupid birds.

Rhetias continued, "Barbers shall wear you on their citterns."

Barbershops contained stringed musical instruments called citterns that customers could play as they waited for service. These citterns resembled a lute and were sometimes decorated with a carving of a grotesque head.

Rhetias continued, "Hucksters will set you out in gingerbread."

People would sell gingerbread men that resembled Cuculus.

"May the Devil take you!" an angry Cuculus said.

He did not want to be mocked, especially in front of nobilities.

He continued, "I say nothing to you now; can't you leave me alone and let me be quiet?"

Loyal to Cuculus, Grilla said to Rhetias, "You're too perstreperous, saucebox."

Grilla meant that he was too noisy.

"Good girl!" Cuculus said. "If we begin to puff once —"

"To puff" means to puff out air as in saying the word "pooh" in a contemptuous tone. More broadly, it meant to speak scornfully or behave scornfully. This was not the place for such talk or behavior.

Pelias said, "Please, hold your tongue; the lords are in the presence."

Nobilities were present, and they were present in the room in which Prince Palador received visitors: the presence chamber.

"Mum, butterfly!" Rhetias replied. "Quiet!"

A butterfly is a foppish courtier.

Seeing Prince Palador, Pelias said, "The prince! Stand and keep quiet."

"Oh, the prince!" Cuculus said.

He said to Grilla, "Wench, you shall see the prince now."

Soft music played, and Prince Palador, holding a book, approached the group.

"Sir!" Sophronos said.

"Gracious sir!" Aretus said.

"Why is there all this company?" Prince Palador asked.

Shocked, Corax said to Prince Palador, "A book! Is this the early exercise I prescribed for you? Instead of pursuing health, which all men covet, you pursue disease.

"Where's your great horse, your hounds, your set at tennis, your game of balloon-ball, the practice of your dancing, your throwing of the hammer, or your learning how to toss a pike?

"All changed into a sonnet!

"Please, sir, grant me free liberty to leave the court. It infects me with the sloth of sleep and excess. In the university I have employments that add profit and report to my profession; here I am lost, and because of your willful dullness I am regarded as a man of neither skill nor honesty.

"You may command my head."

If he wished to, Prince Palador could order an executioner to behead Corax.

Corax continued, "Take it — do!

"It would be better for me to lose my head than to lose my wits, and live in the insane asylum of Bedlam.

"You will force me to live there. I'm almost mad already."

"I believe it," Prince Palador said.

Sophronos said, "Letters have come from Crete that demand a speedy restitution of such ships as by your father were long since detained. If the ships are not speedily returned, the letters threaten defiance."

Aretus said, "These near parts of Syria that unite are now mustering their friends, and by intelligence we learn for certain that the Syrian leader will pretend an ancient interest of tribute intermitted."

The island of Cyprus lay close to Syria, whose leader was now claiming that Cyprus owed long-due tribute that it had not paid.

Sophronos said, "Throughout your land your subjects mutter strangely, and they imagine more than they dare to speak publicly."

"And yet they talk only oddly about you," Corax said.

"Hang them, the mongrels!" Cuculus said.

Courtiers often seek favor through siding with their prince.

"About me!" Prince Palador said. "My subjects talk about me!"

"Yes, and scurvily," Corax said. "And they think worse things, prince, than they speak."

"I'll borrow the patience to listen to these wrongs for a little time," Prince Palador said. "And from the few of you who are here present I will conceive what is the general opinion about me."

Corax thought, *I see! Now he's nettled.*

Prince Palador said, "By all your loves I command you to let me know, without fear or flattery, your thoughts about me and how I am interpreted by you. Speak out boldly."

Sophronos said, "For my part, sir, I will be plain and brief.

"I think you are of nature mild and easy, not willingly provoked, but yet headstrong in any passion that misleads your judgment.

"I think that you are too indulgent in acting on such impulses as spring out of your own inclinations.

"I think that you are too old to be reformed, and yet too young to take fitting counsel from yourself concerning what is most amiss."

"I see!" Prince Palador said.

He then asked Aretus, "Tutor, what is your opinion?"

"I think you dote — with pardon let me say it — too much upon your pleasures, and these pleasures are so wrapped up in self-love that you covet no other change of fortune.

"You want to be still what your birth makes you, but you are loath to toil in such affairs of state as break your sleeps."

In other words, he would rather sleep than tend to his duties as ruler of Cyprus.

Corax said, "I think you want to be by the world reputed a man complete in every point, but you are in manners and in effect indeed a child — a boy, a very boy."

Pelias said, "May it please your grace, I think you contain within yourself the great elixir, soul, and quintessence of all divine perfections. You are the glory of mankind, and the only strict example for earthly monarchs to regulate their lives by.

"You are time's miracle, fame's pride.

"In knowledge, intelligence, sweetness, discourse, weapons, arts —"

Recognizing flattery when he heard it, Prince Palador said, "You are a courtier."

Cuculus said, "But he is not a courtier of the ancient fashion, if it pleases your highness.

"It is I who am that. It is I who am the credit of the court, noble prince; and if you would, by proclamation or letters patent that confer power on me, create me overseer of all the tailors in your dominions, then the golden days — the Golden Age — would appear again.

"Bread would be cheaper, fools would have more intelligence, knaves would have more honesty, and beggars would have more money."

Grilla began, "I think now —"

"Peace, you squall!" Cuculus said.

A squall is a small and/or insignificant person.

Servants — and in this society especially young, female servants — ought not to evaluate a prince, at least to his face.

Prince Palador said to Rhetias, "You have not spoken yet."

"Hang him!" Cuculus said. "He'll do nothing but vehemently criticize and complain."

"Most abominable," Grilla said. "Out upon him! Abolish him!"

"Leave, Cuculus," Corax said quietly. "Follow the lords."

"Stay close, page, stay close behind me," Cuculus said to Grilla. "Don't let yourself be seen."

Corax had arranged previously for everyone to exit quietly without the prince's knowledge so that Rhetias could be alone with Prince Palador.

Everyone quietly exited except Prince Palador and Rhetias.

Prince Palador said, "You are taking somewhat a long time to think."

"I do not think at all," Rhetias replied.

"Am I not worthy of your thought?" Prince Palador asked.

"You are worthy of my pity, but not my reprehension," Rhetias replied.

"Pity!" Prince Palador said.

"Yes, for I pity such to whom I owe service, who exchange their happiness for a misery," Rhetias said.

"Is it a misery to be a prince?" Prince Palador asked.

"Princes who forget their sovereignty, and yield to affected passion, are weary of command," Rhetias said. "You had a father, sir."

"He was your sovereign, while he lived, but what about him?" Prince Palador asked.

"Nothing," Rhetias said. "I only dared to name him; that's all."

Using the royal plural, Prince Palador said, "We order you, by the duty that you owe us, to be plain in what you mean to speak. You know something that we must know. You are free to speak freely. Our ears are open."

"Oh, sir," Rhetias said, "I had rather hold a wolf by the ears than stroke a lion; the greater danger is the last."

Holding a wolf by the ears is dangerous, but being in a position where you can anger a king is worse.

"This is mere trifling," Prince Palador said.

He looked around and said, "Ha! Has everyone stolen away?"

He then said, "We are alone. You have an honest look; you have a tongue, I hope, that is not oiled with flattery. Be open; speak openly.

"Although it is true that in my younger days, when I was a child, I often have heard the name of my father, Agenor, more traduced than I could then observe and completely understand what I was hearing, yet I protest that I never had a friend, a certain friend, who would inform me thoroughly of such errors as often are incident to princes."

"All this may be," Rhetias said. "I have seen a man so curious in feeling the edge of a keen knife that he has cut his fingers. My flesh is not of proof — of proven strength — against the metal I am to handle; my flesh is tenderer than the other."

Rhetias was very aware that speaking openly could anger the prince, and he was very aware that angering a prince is dangerous.

"I see, then, that I must court and persuade you," Prince Palador said. "Take the word of a just prince who tells you now that for anything you speak I have more than a pardon — I have thanks and respect."

Rhetias replied, "I will remind you of an old tale that somewhat concerns you.

"Meleander, the great but unfortunate statesman, was by your father entreated to arrange a match between you and his eldest daughter, the Lady Eroclea. You were both near of an age to be married. I presume you remember a marriage contract, and I presume that you cannot forget her."

"Eroclea was a lovely beauty," Prince Palador said. "Please, continue!"

"Eroclea was brought to court," Rhetias said. "She was courted by your father not for you, Prince Palador, as was learned, but to be made a prey to some less noble design. With your permission, I have forgotten the rest."

Prince Palador's father wanted to make Eroclea his concubine, thereby taking away her virtue and chastity. Rhetias did not want to say anything that would anger the prince.

"Good man, call it back again into your memory," Prince Palador said. "Otherwise, if I lose the remainder of the story, then I am lost, too."

"You persuade me to remember the rest of the story as if you were casting a charm — a spell — on me," Rhetias said. "In brief, a kidnapping of Eroclea by some bad agents was attempted, but the Lord Meleander her father rescued her, and she was conveyed away.

"Meleander was accused of treason, his land was seized, and he himself became mentally disturbed and confined to the castle, where he still lives.

"What would have ensued is unknown, for your father shortly afterward died."

"But what became of fair Eroclea?" Palador asked.

"She has never since been heard of," Rhetias said.

"No hope lives, then, of ever, ever seeing her again?" Prince Palador asked.

"Sir, I was afraid I would anger you," Rhetias said.

The prince was showing emotion.

Rhetias continued, "This was, as I said, an old tale.

"I have now a new one, which may perhaps season the first with a more delightful relish."

"I am prepared to hear your new tale," Prince Palador said. "Say whatever you please."

"My Lord Meleander falling in status, on whose favor my fortunes relied, I furnished myself for travel," Rhetias said, "and I bent my course to Athens; there a pretty incident, after a while, came to my knowledge."

"My ear is open to you," Prince Palador said. "I am listening."

"A young lady engaged to a noble gentleman, as the lady we last mentioned — Eroclea — and your highness were, being hindered by their arguing parents, stole away from her home, and was conveyed disguised as a ship-boy in a merchant ship from the country where she lived, to Corinth first and afterwards to Athens, where in much solitariness she lived, like a youth, almost two years, courted by all for acquaintance, but friend to none by familiarity."

"Was she wearing the clothing of a man?" Prince Palador asked.

"She lived as a handsome young man until, her sweetheart's father having died a year before or more, she received notice of it within the last three months or less, and with much joy returned home, and, as the report in Athens stated, enjoyed the happiness for which she had been long an exile.

"Now, noble sir, if you did love the Lady Eroclea, why may not such safety and fate direct her as directed the other? It is not impossible."

It was not impossible that the Lady Eroclea could return to Cyprus.

"*If* I did love her, Rhetias!" Prince Palador said. "Yes, I did love her.

"Give me your hand."

They shook hands.

Prince Palador continued, "As you served Meleander, and as you are still true to these hands, henceforth serve me."

Rhetias was true to these hands: his hand and Prince Palador's hand. He was true to himself and to his prince.

"My duty and my obedience are my bond, but I have been too bold," Rhetias said.

"Forget the sadder story of my father," Prince Palador said, "and only, Rhetias, learn to read and understand me well. For I must always thank you. You have unlocked a tongue that was vowed to silence; for requital, open the clothing over my chest, Rhetias."

"What do you mean?" Rhetias asked.

"I intend to tie you to an oath of secrecy," Prince Palador said.

Rhetias began to unbutton Prince Palador's shirt, but he was slow and awkward at performing such an action on the clothing of a prince.

"Unfasten the buttons, man," Prince Palador said. "You do it weakly."

After Rhetias had unfastened the buttons and opened the shirt, Prince Palador asked, "What do you find there?"

"A picture in an ornament hung around your neck," Rhetias said.

"Look closely at the picture."

"I am ... yes ... let me observe it," Rhetias said, "The picture is hers, the lady's."

"Whose?" Palador asked.

"Eroclea's," Rhetias said.

"It is the picture of her who was once Eroclea," Palador said.

His way of expressing this acknowledged that Eroclea could well be dead.

Palador continued, "For her sake I have advanced Sophronos to the helm of government. For her sake I will restore Meleander's honors to him. I will, for her sake, beg friendship from you, Rhetias.

"Oh, be faithful, and let no politically minded lord learn from your bosom my griefs. I know you were told to sift me for information, but be not too secure."

Prince Palador had revealed a secret to Rhetias: a secret that he, Prince Palador, did not want to be revealed. Therefore, he was telling Rhetias to be careful and not let any other lord know what he had learned. Palador's words "be not too secure" meant 1) don't be overly confident in your ability to keep a secret, and 2) know that as your prince I can hurt you if you betray my secret.

"I am your creature," Rhetias said.

This meant: I am your devoted subject.

Prince Palador ordered, "Continue still your discontented fashion. Humor the lords, as they would humor me.

"I'll not live in your debt."

This meant: You will be rewarded.

He then said, "We are discovered. Someone is coming."

Amethus, Menaphon, Thamasta, Kala, and Parthenophill entered the scene.

Amethus said, "May honor and health always serve the prince!

"Sir, I am bold — with your permission — to present to your highness my friend Menaphon, who has returned from travel."

"Humbly on my knees I kiss your gracious hand," Menaphon said as he kissed Prince Palador's hand.

"It is our duty to love the virtuous," Prince Palador said.

"If my prayers or service have any value, I vow them to be yours forever," Menaphon said.

"I have a fist for you, too, stripling," Rhetias said, meaning his hand.

He continued, "You have started up prettily — grown — since I last saw you. Have you learned any intelligence abroad? Can you tell news and swear lies with a grace, like a true traveller?"

Travellers were known for telling tall tales about their travels.

Looking at Parthenophill, Rhetias asked, "What new ouzel is this?"

An ouzel is a blackbird. Parthenophill had dark hair.

Thamasta said to Prince Palador, "Your highness shall do right to your own judgment in taking more than common notice of this stranger, an Athenian who is named Parthenophill. He is one who, if my opinion does not flatter me too grossly, deserves a dear respect for the fashion of his mind."

"Your commendations, sweet cousin, speak nobly of him," Palador said.

"May all the supernatural powers that guard just thrones double their guards round about your sacred excellence!" Parthenophill said to Prince Palador.

Prince Palador asked Menaphon, "What fortune led this youth to Cyprus?"

"My persuasions convinced him to come here," Menaphon replied.

Amethus said to Prince Palador, "And if your highness would be pleased to hear the entrance into their first acquaintance, you will say —"

Thamasta interrupted, "— that it was the newest, sweetest, prettiest accidental meeting that ever delighted your attention. I can tell the story of their meeting, sir."

"Some other time," Prince Palador said.

Although he had been told the name earlier, he asked, "What is his name?"

"Parthenophill," Thamasta answered.

"Parthenophill!" Prince Palador said. "We shall arrange time to take more notice of him."

Prince Palador exited.

"His usual melancholy still pursues the prince," Menaphon said.

"I told you so," Amethus said.

"You must not wonder at it," Thamasta said to Parthenophill.

"I do not, lady," Parthenophill replied.

"Shall we go to the castle?" Amethus asked his sister.

"We will accompany you both and render any needed service," Menaphon said.

"We" referred to Menaphon and Parthenophill.

"All three of us will," Rhetias said. "I'll go, too."

He whispered to Amethus, "Listen in your ear, gallant; I'll keep the old madman — Meleander — busy by talking to him, while you gabble to Cleophila, his daughter. My thumb's upon my lips; I'll say not a word about this."

"I need not fear that you will reveal anything you should not, Rhetias," Amethus whispered.

A chance to talk alone to Cleophila necessitated a change in plan. He would tell his sister that he and his male companions would wander the city, giving the impression that they would not go to the castle.

Amethus said out loud, "Sister, expect us soon. Today we will wander the city."

"Well, I shall expect you soon," Thamasta said.

She then whispered to Kala, "Kala!"

Here was a chance for Kala to talk to Parthenophill.

Knowing what Thamasta wanted, Kala replied, "Trust me!"

Rhetias said, "Troop on! Love, love, what a wonder you are!"

Everyone exited except Kala and Parthenophill, whom Kala grabbed by the sleeve and stopped.

"May I not be offensive, sir?" Kala asked. "May I take the liberty of talking to you?"

"What is your pleasure?" Parthenophill said. "What do you want? Yet, please, be brief."

"Then, briefly, good man, tell me this: Do you have a mistress or a wife?" Kala said.

"Mistress" meant a woman he loved but was not married to; it did not imply a woman with whom Parthenophill was having sexual relations.

"I've neither," Parthenophill answered.

"Did you ever love in earnest any fair lady whom you wished to make your own?" Kala asked.

"No, not any, truly," Parthenophill answered.

Kala said, "I will not be inquisitive and ask to know who your friends or what your means are, nor do I care to hope to know those things.

"But suppose that a dowry were thrown down before your choice of woman, a woman of beauty, noble birth, and sincere affection.

"How gladly would you entertain it?

"Young man, I do not tempt you idly."

It sounded as if Kala were proposing to him.

Parthenophill replied, "I shall thank you, when my unsettled thoughts can make me sensible of what it is to be happy.

"As for the present I am your debtor, and fair gentlewoman, please give me permission as yet to study ignorance, for my weak brains don't conceive what concerns me."

In other words, Parthenophill was not sure what was going on: Why was this woman proposing to him?

Beginning to leave, Parthenophill said to Kala, "Some other time."

Coming in as Parthenophill was beginning to leave, Thamasta said, "Am I interrupting your parley, your private conversation, and is that why you are departing?

"Surely, my serving-woman loves you.

"Can she speak well, Parthenophill?"

"Yes, madam," Parthenophill replied. "She can hold a discreetly chaste conversation. She has much won my trust, and in few but pithy words, she has much moved my thankfulness.

"You are her lady. Your goodness aims, I know, at her preferment. Therefore, I may be bold to make a true confession: If I ever desire to thrive in a woman's favor, Kala is the first whom my ambition shall bend to."

"Indeed!" Thamasta said. "But say a nobler love should interpose. Suppose a nobler woman should love you."

Parthenophill replied, "Where real worth and constancy first settle a hearty truth, there greatness cannot shake it; nor shall it shake mine. Yet I am but an infant in that interpretation of Kala's actions and words, which must give clear light to Kala's merit."

Parthenophill had already pledged this: If I ever desire to thrive in a woman's favor, Kala is the first whom my ambition shall bend to. As long as Kala had real worth and constancy, Parthenophill would not go back on this pledge. Parthenophill, however, did not know Kala well, and so he did not know if in fact Kala had real worth and constancy.

He continued, "Riper hours hereafter must teach me how to grow rich in deserts."

In other words, Parthenophill needed to grow older and become wiser. That experience and knowledge would let him know what he deserved. That could be Kala, or it could be Thamasta. Or it could be someone else.

Parthenophill then said, "Madam, my duty waits on you."

That was a way of saying that it was his duty to serve her.

He exited.

"Come here," Thamasta said to Kala. "He said, 'If ever henceforth I desire to thrive in woman's favor, Kala is the first whom my ambition shall bend to.' That's what he said!"

Thamasta was jealous of Kala.

"Those are the very words he spoke," Kala admitted.

"Those very words curse you, unfaithful creature, to your grave," Thamasta said. "You wooed him for yourself!"

"You said I should," Kala replied.

"My name was never mentioned?" Thamasta asked.

"Madam, no," Kala said. "We had not come to that."

Thamasta said, "Not come to that!

"Are you a rival fit to cross my fate?

"Now poverty and a reputation for unchasteness, the waiting-woman's wages, will be your payment, you false, faithless, wanton beast!

"I'll spoil your plans for marriage. There's not a page, a groom, no, not a citizen who shall be cast away upon you, Kala. I'll keep you in my service all your lifetime, without hope of a husband or a suitor."

"Truly, I have not deserved this cruelty," Kala said.

"Parthenophill shall learn, if he respects my birth, the danger of a foolish neglect. He shall learn that he ought not to reject a woman as highly born as I am."

Thamasta exited.

"Are you so quick to anger?" Kala said. "Well, I may chance to cross your peevishness. Now, although I never intended for the young man to be mine, yet, if he should love me, I'll have him, or I'll run away with him, and let her do her worst then!

"What! We're all only flesh and blood; the same thing that will do my lady good will please her serving-woman, too."

Cleophila and Trollio talked together in an apartment at the castle. Cleophila was Meleander's daughter, and Trollio was Meleander's manservant.

"Tread softly, Trollio," Cleophila said. "My father is still sleeping."

"Yes, indeed, he is," Trollio said, "but he sleeps like a hare, with his eyes open, and that's not a good sign."

Hares were thought to be timid creatures that always kept their eyes open in case of the approach of predators.

"Surely, you are weary of this sullen living, but I am not," Cleophila said, "for I find more contentment in my obedience and duty to my father here than in all the delights the time presents elsewhere."

In his room, Meleander groaned.

"Do you hear that groan?" Cleophila asked.

"Hear it!" Trollio said. "I shudder. It was a strong blast, young mistress, able to root up heart, liver, lungs, and all."

"My much-wronged father!" Cleophila said, "Let me see his face."

She drew aside a wall hanging. Behind it was an alcove, in which her father was sitting in a chair and sleeping. His hair and beard were long and unkempt.

"Lady mistress," Trollio said, "shall I fetch a barber to steal away his rough beard while he sleeps? In his naps he never looks in a mirror, and it is high time, and according to reason, for him to be trimmed. He has not been under the shaver's hand during almost the past four years."

Trollio was exaggerating. Meleander's daughter Eroclea had been missing for two years.

"Quiet, fool!" Cleophila said, afraid that he would awaken her father.

Trollio thought, *I could clip the old ruffian; there's hair enough to stuff all the great codpieces in Switzerland.*

A codpiece was a pouch that covered a man's genitals.

Trollio continued thinking, *He begins to stir; he stirs. Bless us, how his eyes roll!*

He then said to Meleander, "May a good year keep your lordship in your right wits, I beseech you!"

By "good year," he meant a lengthy fortuitous time; however, "goodyear" was often used in this society as a euphemism for the Devil.

Meleander called, "Cleophila!"

"Sir, I am here," she replied. "How are you doing, sir?"

"Sir, is your stomach up yet?" Trollio asked. "Are you hungry? Get some warm porridge in your belly; it is very good at settling brains."

Imagining his daughter Eroclea's funeral, Meleander said, "The raven croaked, and hollow shrieks of owls sung dirges at her funeral; I laughed all the while, for it was useless to weep. The girl was fresh and full of youth: but, oh, the cunning of tyrants, who look big! Their very frowns judge poor souls guilty even before their case is heard."

He then asked Trollio and Cleophila, "Good people, who are you, and who are you?"

"I am Cleophila, your woeful daughter."

"I am Trollio, your honest implement."

An "implement" is an instrument; Trollio meant servant.

"I know you both," Meleander said.

He then said to Cleophila, "Alas, why do you treat me like this? Your sister, my Eroclea, was so gentle that young turtledoves — which completely lack spleens that produce gall — in their downy feathers nourish more gall than her spleen had ever mixed with, yet, when winds and storms drive dirt and dust on banks of spotless snow, the purest whiteness is no such defense against the sullying foulness of that fury.

"So raved Agenor, that great man, evil against the girl. It was a malicious, cunning trick!"

Agenor was Prince Palador's father, who had coveted Eroclea for himself after arranging for Prince Palador and Eroclea's engagement.

Meleander continued, "We were too old in honor."

He meant that he had been so accustomed to dealing with honorable men that he was unprepared for Agenor's evil designs on Eroclea.

Meleander continued, "I am lean, and fallen away extremely. I have lost weight, and most assuredly I have not dined these past three days."

"Will you eat now, sir?" Cleophila asked.

"I beseech you heartily to eat, sir," Trollio said. "I feel a horrible puking myself."

He was saying that he did not feel well; it is likely he thought that some food would settle his stomach.

"Am I stark mad?" Meleander asked.

Trollio thought, *No, no, you are only a little staring; there's a difference between staring and stark mad. You are but whimsied yet — crotcheted, conundrumed, or so on. You are only filled with odd notions.*

Meleander said, "Here's all my worry, and I often sigh for you, Cleophila; we are secluded from all good people.

"But be careful: Amethus is the son of Doryla, Agenor's sister. There's some ill blood about him, if the surgeons have not been very skillful and let the ill blood all out."

Doctors engaged in bloodletting as a health measure.

"I am, alas, too grieved to think of love," Cleophila said. "Romantic love must concern me least."

"Sirrah, be wise!" Meleander said. "Be wise!"

A man of a higher social class would sometimes address a man of a lower social class by the title "sirrah."

"Who, I?" Trollio asked. "I will be monstrous and wise immediately."

Amethus, Menaphon, Parthenophill, and Rhetias entered the room.

"Welcome, gentlemen," Trollio said. "The more the merrier. I'll lay the cloth, and set the stools in readiness, for I see that there is some hope of dinner now."

He exited.

Amethus said, "My Lord Meleander, your kinsman Menaphon, newly returned from travel, comes to tender his duty to you."

He then said to Cleophila, "And he comes to tender his love to you, fair mistress."

Menaphon said to Meleander, "I wish that I could as easily remove sadness from your memory, sir, as study to do you faithful service."

He then said to Cleophila, "My dear cousin, may all the best of comforts bless your sweet obedience!"

She was treating her father well and taking care of him.

Cleophila replied, "One of the chief of my best of comforts, worthy cousin, lives in you and your well-doing."

Menaphon said about Parthenophill, "This young stranger will well deserve your knowledge and acquaintanceship."

"For my friend's sake, lady, please give him welcome," Amethus requested.

"He has met my welcome, if a person with sorrows can look kindly," Cleophila replied.

"You much honor me," Parthenophill said.

Looking at Meleander, Rhetias thought, *How he eyes the company! Surely my passionate feelings will betray my weakness.*

Rhetias had served Meleander before Meleander began to suffer from misfortunes and mental illness. The sight of him caused Rhetias' gentler feelings to rise up, threatening to expose his cynical façade as merely a pose.

Rhetias said to Meleander, "Oh, my master, my noble master, do not forget me. I am still the humblest and the most faithful in heart of those who serve you."

Meleander laughed.

Rhetias thought, *There's bitter wormwood in that laughter; it is the usher to a violent extreme.*

"I am a weak old man," Meleander said. "All these people have come to jeer at my ripe calamities."

"Good uncle!" Menaphon said.

"But I'll outstare you all," Meleander said. "Fools, desperate fools!

"You're cheated, grossly cheated; range, range on, and roll about the world to gather moss, the moss of honor, gay reports, gay clothes, gay wives, and huge empty buildings whose proud roofs shall with their pinnacles even reach the stars.

"You work and work like blind moles in the paths that are bored through the crannies of the earth, in order to charge your hungry souls with such full surfeits as, once being gorged, make you lean with plenty.

"And when you have skimmed the vomit of your riots, you're fat in no felicity but folly."

"Skimmed the vomit" is like "skimmed the fat from whole milk." Those fools who skim the vomit of riotous living and consume it grow fat in no happiness but foolishness.

This can mean to grow fat in no happiness except the happiness that is foolishness.

Or this can mean to grow fat in no happiness at all but instead to grow fat in foolishness.

Meleander continued, "Then your last sleeps seize on you in the grave, and then the troops of worms crawl around and feast on your corpses: merriment, rich fare, dainty, delicious!

"Here's Cleophila; she is all the poor stock of my remaining thrift.

"You, you, the prince's cousin, how do you like her? Amethus, how do you like her?"

Amethus replied, "My intentions are just and honorable."

"Sir, believe him," Menaphon said.

"Take her," Meleander said. "We two must part." He said to Cleophila, "Go to him, do."

"This sight is full of horror," Parthenophill said.

"There is sense still in this distraction," Rhetias said.

Meleander said, "In this jewel I have given away all that I can call mine. When I am dead, save on expenses. Let me be buried in a nook with no guns of honor, no pompous whining — these are fooleries.

"If we — while we live — stalk about the streets jostled by cart-men, foot-messengers, and fine apes in silken coats, neglected and scarcely thought about, then it is not comely for us to be drawn to the earth for burial dressed in antique and fantastic trappings like well-fed jades upon a day for tilts and jousts."

In other words, if we live ordinary lives without suffering great harm, we ought not to be indulged with a fancy funeral after we die.

Meleander said, "Scorn to useless tears!"

This can mean, "Show scorn to useless tears!"

Tears won't help, so don't shed them.

Or it can mean: "Scorn to use less [fewer] tears."

Shed many, many tears, especially at the funeral of a person such as Eroclea.

Meleander continued, "Eroclea was not coffined in such a way; she perished, and no eye dropped tears except mine and I am childish. I talk like one who dotes. Laugh at me, Rhetias, or rail at me and shout at me.

"They will not give me food."

Literally, that was not true, but Cleophila and Trollio were not able to give him the kind of metaphorical food he wanted: He wanted Eroclea back.

Meleander continued, "They've starved me, but I'll henceforth be my own cook.

"Good morning! It is too early for me to revel with you because of my cares; I will break my heart a little, and tell you more hereafter.

"Please be merry."

He exited.

"I'll follow him," Rhetias said.

He whispered, "My Lord Amethus, use your time with Cleophila carefully. Few words soonest prevail as long as they are to the purpose. Make no long orations. Speak plainly and briefly."

He said again out loud, "I'll follow him."

He exited.

Amethus said, "Cleophila, although these blacker clouds of sadness thicken and make dark the sky of your fair eyes, yet give me permission to follow the stream of my affections: They are pure, without any mixture of ignoble thoughts.

"Can you ever be mine?"

"I am so low in my own fortunes and my father's woes, that I lack words to tell you that you deserve a worthier choice than I," Cleophila replied.

"But give me permission to hope," Amethus requested.

"My friend is serious," Menaphon said.

"Sir, accept this for your answer," Cleophila said. "If I ever thrive in any earthly happiness, second to my good father's wished-for recovery must be my thankfulness to your great merit. This much I dare promise.

"You cannot urge more from me at the present time."

Meleander called from another room, "Cleophila!"

"This gentleman is moved by strong emotion," Cleophila said about Parthenophill.

"Your eyes, Parthenophill, are guilty of showing some grief," Amethus said. "You are weeping."

"Friend, what ails you?" Menaphon asked.

"All is not well within me, sir," Parthenophill replied.

"Cleophila!" Meleander called again.

"Sweet maiden, don't forget me," Amethus said. "We now must part."

"Always you shall have my prayers for you," Cleophila said.

"Always you will have my loyalty," Amethus said.

CHAPTER 3

— 3.1 —

Cuculus and Grilla talked together in a room in the palace. Cuculus was wearing a black velvet cap and a white feather, and he was holding a paper in his hand.

Cuculus asked, "Don't I look freshly, and like a youth of the finest trim? Don't I look fashionably dressed like a young person?"

"You look like as rare an old youth as ever walked cross-gartered," Grilla said.

At this time, cross-garters were regarded as old-fashioned.

"Here are my mistresses mustered in white and black," Cuculus said. He had written down the names of the women he intended to pursue.

He read out loud, "*Kala, the waiting-woman.*"

Then he said, "I will first begin at the foot."

Kala had the lowest social class of the three women he intended to pursue.

He then said to Grilla, "Let's play-act. You take the role of Kala."

"I stand in for Kala," Grilla said. "Do your best and your worst."

"I must look haughty, and care little or nothing for her, because she is a creature that stands at livery," Cuculus said.

Livery is the uniform of a servant, but a livery stable is also a stable for horses that are hired out. Women who are hired out may be servants — or whores.

Cuculus continued, "Thus I talk wisely, and to no purpose."

He then addressed Grilla, who was pretending to be Kala, "Wench, as it is not fitting that you should be either fair or honest, so, considering your service, you are as you are, and so are your betters, let them be what they can be."

He was being insulting.

Cuculus continued, "Thus, in despite and defiance of all your good parts, if I cannot endure your baseness, it is more out of your courtesy than my deserving; and so I expect your answer."

He was being nonsensical.

Grilla said, "I must confess —"

Cuculus interrupted, "Well said."

Grilla said, "You are —"

Cuculus interrupted, "That's true, too."

"To describe you rightly, you are a very scurvy fellow," Grilla said.

"Go away! Go away!" Cuculus said. "Do you think so?"

"You are a very foul-mouthed and misshapen coxcomb," Grilla said.

"I'll never believe it, I swear by this hand of mine," Cuculus said.

Grilla said, "You are a maggot, most unworthy to creep in to the least wrinkle of a gentlewoman's —"

Then Grilla stopped and thought.

While Grilla thinks, the reader may think of the wrinkles — wavy folds — of a gentlewoman's ... labia minora, perhaps.

In this society, one meaning of "wrinkle" is "moral fault."

Unable to think of the word or words she (or he) wanted, Grilla asked, "What do you call good conceit, or so, or whatever you will else?"

She then continued, "— were you not refined by courtship and education, which in my bleary eyes makes you appear as sweet as any nosegay, or savory bag of musk newly fallen from the civet cat."

The scent of a new bag of musk fallen from a civet cat is strong and repulsive; the musk must be diluted before it can be used to make perfume.

Cuculus said, "This shall serve well enough for Kala the waiting-woman.

"My next mistress is Cleophila, the old madman's daughter. I must come to her in whining tune. I must sigh, wipe my eyes, fold my arms, and blubber out my speech like this:

"*Even as a kennel of hounds, sweet lady, cannot catch a hare when they are filled up with the carrion of a dead horse —*"

Yuck.

He continued, "— *so, even so, the gorge of my affections being fully crammed with the garboils of your condolements does tickle me with the prick, as it were, about me, and fellow-feeling of howling outright.*"

In other, perhaps better words, "— similarly, my being affected by the hubbub of your lamentations makes me want to weep and even howl out of sympathy for your suffering."

"This will do it, if we will hear it," Grilla said.

"We" meant both Cleophila and Grilla (because Grilla was performing the role of Cleophila). Grilla was hinting, however, that Cleophila was likely to ignore Cuculus and not hear what he had to say.

Cuculus said, "You see I am crying ripe tears — they are actually trickling down my face — I am such another tender-hearted fool."

Grilla said, "Even as the snuff of a candle that is burnt in the socket goes out, and leaves a strong perfume behind it; or as a piece of toasted cheese next to the heart in a morning is a restorative for a sweet breath —"

Eating a piece of toasted cheese in the morning can restore pleasant-smelling breath — assuming those around you like the scent of toasted cheese.

She continued, "— even so, the odoriferous savor of your love does perfume my heart" — she sighed — "with the pure scent of an intolerable content, and is not to be endured."

Grilla was a good-enough actress that Cuculus thought that what she had said was complimentary.

He said, "I swear by this hand of mine, this play-acting is excellent!

"Be prepared to tackle, last of all, the role of the Princess Thamasta, she who is my mistress — my lady-boss — indeed. She is abominably proud, a lady of a damnably high, turbulent, and generous spirit, but I have a loud-mouthed cannon of my own to batter her, and a penned speech of purpose: Observe it."

Talking about performing the role of Thamasta, Grilla said, "Thus I walk by, hear your speech, and pay no attention to you."

Cuculus read out loud, "*Though haughty as the devil or his dam you do appear, great mistress, yet I am similar to an ugly firework, and can mount above the region of your sweet ac count.*"

He verbally stumbled while reading "*account*," mispronouncing "*count*," while barely pronouncing "*ac*," with the result that he sounded as if he were talking about Thamasta's "sweet cunt."

Cuculus continued, "*Were you the moon herself, yet having seen you, behold the man ordained to move within you.*"

The "move" could be a moving of emotion within her, or a moving of a penis within her.

He then said to Grilla, "Look to yourself, housewife! Answer me in strong poetic lines — you had best do it."

"Housewife" meant "Grilla," but the "strong poetic lines" were those that Grilla would come up with while play-acting the role of Thamasta.

"Keep away, poor fool — my beams will strike you blind," Grilla said. "Else, if you touch me, touch me but behind."

It sounded as if she were inviting him to touch her butt.

Grilla continued, "In palaces, such as pass in before must be great princes; for at the back-door tatterdemalions wait, who know not how to get admittance — such a one are you."

Hmm. The literal meaning is clear, but the bawdy meaning is this: In palaces (ladies' crotches), princes can use the front door (the vagina), but lower-class tatterdemalions are waiting at the back door (the anus) because they don't know how to achieve penetration — and Cuculus is one of those tatterdemalions.

"By God's foot, this is downright roaring language," Cuculus said. "These are fighting words."

"I know how to present a big lady in her own disposition," Grilla said. "But, please, seriously, are you in love with all these ladies?"

A big lady is a lady of high status.

"Pish!" Cuculus said. "I have not a rag of love about me; it is only a foolish mood I am possessed with, to be surnamed the Conqueror. I will court anything, but I will be in love with nothing, nor no thing."

A thing is a penis; no thing is a vulva.

"A rare man you are, I declare," Grilla said.

"Yes, I know I am a rare man, and I have always regarded myself as such," Cuculus said.

Pelias the foolish courtier and Corax the doctor entered the room.

Looking at Cuculus and Grilla, Pelias said, "In amorous contemplation, I swear on my life. He is courting his page, by Helicon!"

Mount Helicon in Greece is sacred to the Muses.

"That is false," Cuculus said.

"It is a gross untruth," Grilla said. "I'll back up what I say, sir, at any time, in any place, with any weapon."

"Indeed, she shall," Cuculus said.

"No quarrels, Goody Whisk!" Corax said to Grilla, calling her a whipper-snapper.

He then said, "Set aside your trifling, and fall to your practice. Instructions are ready for you all. Pelias is your leader; follow him. Get credit now or never. Vanish, you doodles, vanish!"

"Are you talking about the performance we must prepare to deliver?" Cuculus asked.

"The same," Corax said. "Get you gone, and make no bawling."

Everyone except Corax exited.

Corax said to himself, "To waste my time thus, like a drone, in the court, and lose so many hours as my studies have hoarded up, is to be like a man who creeps both on his hands and knees to climb a mountain's top, a place where, when he has ascended it, one careless slip tumbles him down again into the bottom, from where he first began.

"I need no prince's favor; princes need my skill. So then, Corax, be no more a fool. The best of them cannot fool you, no, they shall not."

Sophronos, one of the prince's counselors, and Aretus, the prince's tutor, entered the room.

"We have found the doctor at a good time now; from him let's learn the cause," Sophronos said.

"It is fitting we should," Aretus replied.

He then said to Doctor Corax, "Sir, we know that you are learned, and, since your skill can best discern the humors that are predominant in bodies subject to alteration, tell us, please, what devil this disease called Melancholy is, which can transform men into monsters."

This society existed before the age of modern medicine. Doctors in this society believed that the human body had four humors, or vital fluids. Each humor made a contribution to the personality, and for a human being to be sane and healthy, the four humors had to be present in the right amounts. If a man had too much of a certain humor, it would harm his personality and health.

Blood was the sanguine humor. A sanguine man was optimistic.

Phlegm was the phlegmatic humor. A phlegmatic man was calm.

Yellow bile was the choleric humor. A choleric man was angry.

Black bile was the melancholic humor. A melancholic man was gloomy.

When a man was ill, doctors would try to get the four humors back into balance by purging him, often through bloodletting or through the use of laxatives.

Corax' view of Melancholy differed from the conventional wisdom.

Corax said, "You are yourself a scholar, and quick of understanding. Melancholy is not, as you conceive, indisposition of body, but is instead the mind's disease. So Ecstasy, Fantastic Dotage, Madness, Frenzy, Rapture of Mere Imagination, differ partly from Melancholy, which is briefly this:

"A mere commotion of the mind, overcharged with fear and sorrow, first begotten in the brain, the seat of reason, and from there derived as suddenly into the heart, the seat of our affection."

Aretus asked, "Are there various kinds of this disturbance?"

"An infinite number," Corax said. "It would be easier to prognosticate every hour we have to live than reckon up the kinds or causes of this anguish of the mind."

Sophronos said, "Thus you conclude that, as the cause is doubtful, then the cure must be impossible, and so then our Prince Palador, poor gentleman, is lost forever as well to himself as to his subjects."

"My lord, you are too quick to conclude that I think that," Corax said. "Thus much I dare to promise and do; before many minutes pass I will discover from where his sadness comes, or I will undergo the censure of my ignorance."

"You are a noble scholar," Aretus said.

"You shall make your own demand for your reward," Sophronos said.

"May I be sure of that?" Corax said.

"We both will pledge our truth," Aretus said. "Sophronos and I both pledge that what Sophronos said is true."

"What I promised to do will be soon performed," Corax said, "and what I want is that I may be discharged from my attendance at court, and never anymore be sent for afterward. Or if I am sent for, may rats gnaw all my books, if I once get home, and come here again!

"Although my neck may stretch a halter for my not coming when sent for, I don't care. Let me be hung if I come here again."

A halter is a noose.

"Come, come, you shall not fear it," Sophronos said.

"I'll tell you what is to be done, and you shall make it ready to happen," Corax said.

Kala and Parthenophill talked together in a room in Thamasta's house.

Kala said, "My lady is expecting you — she thinks all time moves too slowly until you come to her. Therefore, young man, if you intend to love me, and me only, then before we part, without more circumstance, let us betroth ourselves. Let's get engaged to be married."

"I dare not wrong you," Parthenophill said. "You are too violent."

"Wrong me no more than I wrong you," Kala said. "Be mine, and I am yours. I cannot be concerned about picky points."

"Then, to resolve all further hopes, you never can be mine," Parthenophill said. "You must not, and pardon me although I say you shall not."

Kala thought, *The thing is surely a gelding! He must have been castrated if he rejects me!*

"Shall not!" she said. "Well, you had best prate to my lady now, what offer I have made to you. Tell her that I asked you to marry me."

"Never, I vow," Parthenophill said.

"Do! Do!" Kala said. "It is but a kind heart of my own, and ill luck can undo me."

She meant that her kind heart had made her fancy Parthenophill, but her ill luck in choosing him could ruin her.

She thought, *I am refused and rejected! Oh, scurvy!*

Kala then said, "Please walk on. I'll catch up with you."

Parthenophill exited

"What a green-sickness-livered boy Parthenophill is!" she said.

The disease called green sickness, which is known today as hypochromic anemia, sometimes afflicted young girls in this society. The disease gave the sufferer's skin a greenish tint.

Kala, of course, was saying that Parthenophill was much more like a young woman than a man because he had rejected her.

She continued, "My maidenhead will shortly grow so stale that it will be moldy, but I'll mar Thamasta's market — I'll ruin her chance of marrying Parthenophill."

Menaphon entered the room and said, "Parthenophill passed this way. Please, Kala, tell me where I can find him."

"Yes, I can tell you," Kala said. "But you, sir, must have patience with him."

"Have patience!" Menaphon said.

"That's what I said," Kala replied. "Your excellence has engaged my loyalty. Learn a secret that will, as you are a man, startle your reason. It is only the respect of what I owe to thankfulness and my gratitude for you.

"Dear sir, the stranger whom your courtesy received as a friend has become your rival."

"Rival, Kala!" Menaphon said. "Take heed. Be careful. You are too credulous."

"My lady Thamasta dotes on and loves Parthenophill," Kala said. "I will place you in a room where, although you cannot hear, yet you shall see such interactions between the two as will confirm the truth of what I have told you."

"It will make me mad," Menaphon said.

"Yes, yes," Kala said. "It makes me mad, too, that a gentleman so excellently sweet, so liberal, so kind, so proper, should be so betrayed by a young smooth-chinned interloper, but, for love's sake, bear everything with manly courage. Don't say a word; if you reveal that I have told you this, then I would be ruined."

"That would be much too pitiful," Menaphon said. "Honest, most honest Kala, your care, your serviceable care for me, is why you have told me this."

"You have even spoken all that can be said or thought about my motives," Kala replied.

"I will reward you," Menaphon said. "But as for him, that ungentle boy, I'll whip his falsehood with a vengeance."

"Oh, speak quietly," Kala said. "Walk up these stairs and take this key with you; it opens a chamber-door, where, at that window yonder, you may see all their courtship."

Menaphon said, "I am silent."

"Make as little noise as you can, I beg you," Kala said. "There is a back-stair to convey you from here unseen and unsuspected."

Menaphon exited.

Alone, Kala said to herself, "He — Parthenophill — who cheats a waiting-woman of a free good session of sex she longs for must expect a shrewd revenge. Sheep-spirited boy! Although he had not married me, he might have proffered sexual kindness in a corner, and never have been the worse for it.

"I see them coming here. On goes my set of faces most demurely. I will use expressions that show that I am loyal and honest."

Thamasta and Parthenophill entered the room. Unseen, Menaphon watched from a window.

Thamasta ordered Kala, "Leave the room."

"Yes, madam," Kala replied.

"Whoever demands access to me, deny him entrance until I call you; and wait outside."

"I shall," Kala said.

She thought, *Sweet Venus, turn his sexual vigor into a snowball! I heartily beg it!*

She wanted Parthenophill to reject Thamasta just as he had rejected her. Kala exited.

Thamasta said, "I expose the honor of my birth, my fame, my youth, to the risk of much unfavorable interpretation, in seeking an adventure of a parley, so private, with a stranger."

In this society, an upper-class woman would not be alone with a man who was not her husband or biological relative. She would always be accompanied by a female chaperone. Thamasta was risking much gossip by having a private conversation with Parthenophill.

She continued, "If your thoughts do not judge me with mercy, you may soon believe I have laid by that modesty that should preserve unstained a virtuous name."

Parthenophill replied, "Lady, to shorten long excuses, time and safe experience have so thoroughly armed my understanding with a real taste of your most noble nature, that to question the least part of your bounties, or that freedom which heaven has aplenty made you rich in, would be evidence that I am incivil and lacking in manners, and what is more, basely bred, and which is most of all, unthankful."

Thamasta then listed several examples of attraction found in nature:

"The constant magnet and the steel are found in separate mines, yet there is such a league between these minerals that it is as if one vein of earth had nourished both.

"The gentle myrtle is not grafted upon an olive tree's stock, yet nature has between them locked a secret of sympathy, so that, if they are planted near each other, they will, both in their branches and their roots, embrace each other.

"Twines of ivy round the well-grown oak.

"The vine courts the elm.

"Yet all of these are different plants."

She then said, "Parthenophill, if you consider rightly what I have said, then these slight creatures will fortify the reasons I should frame for that ungrounded — as you might think — affection that is submitted to a stranger's pity.

"True love may blush, when shame repents too late, but in all actions nature yields to fate."

Thamasta was saying that her attraction for Parthenophill was like a magnet's attraction for steel, and et cetera in the other examples she had mentioned. She admitted that she had not acted as their society would dictate, but her excuse was the necessity of acting on her love — that was her fate.

Parthenophill replied, "Great lady, it would be a dullness that must exceed the grossest and most stupid kind of ignorance not to be sensible of your intentions — I clearly understand them. Yet the difference between that height and lowness which does distinguish our unequal fortunes so much dissuades me from ambition that I am humbler in my desires than love's own power can any way raise up."

He was saying the difference in his and Thamasta's social ranks kept him from being ambitious to be with her.

"I am a princess, and I acknowledge no law of slavery," Thamasta said. "To sue for love, yet be denied!"

As a princess, Thamasta rejected being a slave. She was not one to plead for something and yet be refused it.

Parthenophill, who regarded virtue highly, said, "I am so much a subject to every law of noble honesty that to transgress the vows of my perfect friendship to Menaphon I regard as a sacrilege as foul and cursed as if some holy temple had been robbed, and I were the thief."

"You are unwise, young man, to enrage a lioness," Thamasta said.

"It would be unjust to falsify a faith, and forever after, disrobed of that fair ornament, live naked as a scorn to time and truth," Parthenophill said.

"Remember well who I am, and what you are," Thamasta said.

"That remembrance prompts me to perform worthy duty," Parthenophill said. "Oh, great lady, if some few days have tempted your noble heart to cast away affection on a stranger, if that affection has so overpowered your judgment that it, in a manner, has debased your sovereignty of birth and spirit, then how can you turn your eyes away from that looking-glass wherein you may newly trim and settle right a memorable name?"

The "looking-glass" was Menaphon. We look in a looking-glass or mirror in order to improve our appearance; by fixing her gaze on Menaphon rather than on Parthenophill, Thamasta could improve her name, which was already memorable. She could improve her name by marrying Menaphon.

"The youth is idle," Thamasta said. "He is out of his senses."

Parthenophill said, "Days, months, and years have passed since Menaphon has loved and served you truly.

"Menaphon is a man of no large distance in his rank from yours; you and he both have high birth. In qualities he is deserving. He is graced with youth, experience, and every happy gift that can by nature or by education improve a gentleman.

"Great lady, let me be successful in my pleading for him, so that you will yet at last unlock the bounty that your love and care have wisely treasured up and enrich his life."

Thamasta replied sarcastically, "You have a moving — persuasive — eloquence, Parthenophill!"

She added, "Parthenophill, in vain we strive to cross the destiny that guides us. My great heart is stooped so much beneath that accustomed pride that first disguised it that I now prefer a miserable life with you before all other earthly comforts."

"Menaphon, through me, repeats the self-same words to you," Parthenophill said. "You are too cruel, if you can distrust his truth or my report."

Thamasta said, "Go where you will. I'll be an exile with you. I will learn to bear all change of fortunes."

"I plead with grounds of reason for my friend," Parthenophill said. "I am arguing rationally, not emotionally."

Thamasta replied, "For your love, hard-hearted youth, I here renounce all thoughts of other hopes, of other relationships."

"Stop, as you honor virtue," Parthenophill said.

Thamasta began, "When the proffers of other greatness —"

Parthenophill interrupted, "Lady!"

Thamasta continued, "When the entreaties of friends —"

Parthenophill interrupted, "I'll ease your grief."

Thamasta continued, "Respect of kindred —"

Parthenophill interrupted, "Please, listen to me."

Thamasta continued, "Loss of reputation —"

Parthenophill interrupted, "I ask for only a few minutes."

Thamasta continued, "— shall infringe my vows, let Heaven —"

Parthenophill interrupted, "My love speaks to you. Listen, and then go on speaking."

"Your love!" Thamasta said. "Why, your love is a charm that will stop a vow in its most violent course."

Parthenophill said, "Cupid has broken his arrows here, and, like an unarmed child, he has come to make sport between us with no weapon but feathers stolen from his mother's doves."

Cupid, the son of Venus, to whom doves are sacred, is known for shooting arrows that make a person fall in love with another person.

"This is mere trifling," Thamasta said.

"Lady, know a secret," Parthenophill said. "I am as you are — in a lower rank else of the self-same sex — a maiden, a virgin."

In this society, a young male virgin could be called a maiden; however, Parthenophill was saying that he was of the self-same sex as Thamasta — in other words, Parthenophill was a she and not a he. Parthenophill did not say why he — this book will continue to refer to Parthenophill as a he — was dressed in male clothing and pretending to be a man.

Parthenophill continued, "And now, to use your own words, 'If your thoughts do not judge me with mercy, you may soon believe I have laid by that modesty that should preserve a virtuous name unstained.'"

"Are you not a man, then?" Thamasta asked.

Parthenophill replied, "When you shall read the story of my sorrows, with the change of my misfortunes, in a letter recording my true account of my life, I believe you will not think the shedding of one tear a prodigality that misbecomes your pity and my fortune."

Parthenophill would write that letter and see that Thamasta received it.

"Please, conceal the errors of my passion," Thamasta said.

Parthenophill replied, "I wish I had much more of honor ... as for life, I don't value it ... to presume on your secrecy!"

He would conceal the errors of Thamasta's passion, and he wished he had much more of honor so that she would not feel she had to ask him to conceal the errors of her passion.

Thamasta said, "It will be a hard task for my reason to relinquish the affection that was once devoted to you. I shall for a while still consider you the youth I loved so dearly."

"You shall find me always your ready and faithful servant," Parthenophill said.

"Oh, the powers who direct our hearts laugh at our follies!" Thamasta said. "We must not part yet."

"Don't let my unworthiness alter your good opinion," Parthenophill replied.

"I shall henceforth be jealous of your company with any other person," Thamasta said. "My fears are strong and many."

Kala entered the room and asked, "Did your ladyship call me?"

"What for?" Thamasta asked.

"Your servant Menaphon desires admittance into the room," Kala said.

Thamasta had previously recognized Menaphon as her devoted servant — that is, as someone who loved her, and someone who was her wooer.

Without permission, Menaphon entered the room and said, "Pardon me, great mistress, I have come."

He said, "So private! Is this well, Parthenophill?"

Parthenophill began, "Sir, noble sir —"

Menaphon interrupted, "You are unkind and treacherous. This is what happens when you trust a straggler!"

A straggler is a vagabond.

Thamasta began, "Please, servant —"

Menaphon interrupted, "I dare not question you; you are my mistress, my prince's nearest kinswoman, but he —"

Thamasta interrupted, "Come, you are angry."

Menaphon said, "Henceforth I will bury unmanly passion in perpetual silence. I'll court my own distraction, dote on folly, creep to the mirth and madness of the age, rather than be so enslaved again to Woman, which in her best of constancy is steadiest in change and scorn."

He now disliked women in general.

"How dare you talk to me like this!" Thamasta said.

"Dare!" Menaphon said. "If you weren't the sister of my friend, the sister of my friend Amethus, I would hurl you as far away from my eyes as from my heart; for I would never again look at you.

"Take your jewel — Parthenophill — to you!

"And, youth, keep under her wing so she can protect you, or … boy! … boy!"

He was now so angry he could not finish the sentence.

Thamasta said, "If my commands have no force, then let me entreat you, Menaphon."

Menaphon said, "It is for naught. It is useless. Your entreaty is worthless."

In this society, the word "naught" also meant "wickedness."

He then said, "Damn, damn, Parthenophill! Have I deserved to be treated like this?"

Parthenophill began, "I do protest —"

Menaphon interrupted, "You shall not. Henceforth I will be free and hate my bondage."

Amethus entered the room and said, "Go, go to the court! Prince Palador is pleased to see a masque tonight. We must attend on him. It is close to the time for the masque. How thrives your love suit?"

"The judge, your sister, will decide it shortly," Menaphon said.

Thamasta said, "Parthenophill, I will not trust you to be away from me."

She wanted him near her so she could protect him from Menaphon's anger.

Prince Palador, Sophronos, Aretus, and Corax were talking together in a room in the palace. Servants carrying torches were present. Corax was carrying a paper that listed the parts of the masque: Each part presented a type of melancholia.

"Lights," Corax ordered. "Attendance!"

By "Attendance!" he meant, "Pay attention!"

Corax then said, "I will show your highness a trifle that has come from my own brain. If you can, imagine you are now at the university. If you can, you'll take this trifle well enough; it is a scholar's fancy, a quab. It is nothing other than a very quab."

A quab is literally a marsh or bog in which water and earth are mixed; figuratively, it is something formless and without definite shape. A quab is also an unfledged bird: one that is not fully mature.

"We will see it," Prince Palador said.

"Yes, and grace it, too, sir," Sophronos said. "For Corax will otherwise be moody and testy."

"By all means," Aretus said. "Men singular in skill — distinguished in learning — always have some odd whimsy more than is usual."

"What is the name of this masque?" Prince Palador asked.

"Sir, it is called 'The Masque of Melancholy,'" Corax answered.

"We must look for nothing but sadness and seriousness in this masque here, then," Aretus said.

Corax said, "Rather, you must look for madness in several varieties. Melancholy is the root as well of every apish — foolish or affected — frenzy, laughter, and mirth, just as it is the root of dullness."

He then gave the paper he was holding to Prince Palador and said, "Please, my lord, hold this, and observe the plot. What the masque shall now express in action is in this paper expressed in its essential nature."

Amethus, Menaphon, Thamasta, and Parthenophill entered the room.

"Make no interruption," Corax said. "Take your places quickly."

Amethus, Menaphon, Thamasta, and Parthenophill began to bow and curtsey to Prince Palador, but Corax said, "No, no, there's no need and time for ceremony now."

He then ordered, "Sound to announce the entrance!"

A trumpet sounded, and the masque began.

First, Rhetias appeared in character as a person suffering from the type of Melancholia called Lycanthropia. His face had been whited with makeup, he was wearing black shaggy hair and long fingernails, and he was carrying a piece of raw meat.

"Bow wow! Bow wow!" Rhetias barked. "The moon's eclipsed. I'll go to the churchyard and sup. Since I turned into a wolf, I bark, and I howl, and I dig up graves. I will never have the sun shine again. It is midnight, deep dark midnight. Get a prey, and fall to — I have catched you now!"

He growled.

Corax explained, "This kind of Melancholy is called Lycanthropia, sir. It occurs when men believe themselves to be wolves."

Prince Palador looked at the paper Corax had given him and said, "Here I find it."

Second, Pelias entered, wearing a grotesque crown of feathers. Possibly, the feathers formed two horns. He was portraying a man afflicted with Hydrophobia, or Rabies.

Pelias said, "I will hang them all, and burn my wife. Was I not an emperor? My hand was kissed, and ladies lay down before me. In triumph I rode with my nobles about me until the mad dog bit me: I fell, and I fell, and I fell.

"It shall be treason by statute for any man to say the word 'water' or wash his hands, throughout all my dominions.

"Break all the looking-glasses! I will not see my horns: My wife cuckolds me — she is a whore, a whore, a whore, a whore!"

He was referring to the invisible horns that cuckolds — men with unfaithful wives — were said to have growing out of their heads.

Prince Palador said, "Hydrophobia is what you call this?"

Corax said, "Yes, and men so possessed shun all sight of water. Sometimes, if Hydrophobia is mixed with jealousy, it renders them incurable, and often brings death."

Third, a man portraying a Philosopher entered. He was wearing black rags, with a copper chain around his neck, and an old gown half off, and he was carrying a book. The Philosopher was portraying Delirium.

The Philosopher said, "Philosophers dwell in the moon. Speculation and theory girdle the world about like a wall. Ignorance, like an atheist, must be damned in the pit. I am very, very poor, and poverty is the medicine for the soul: My opinions are pure and perfect. Envy is a monster, and I defy the beast."

Corax said, "This is called Delirium, which is mere dotage, sprung from ambition first and singularity, self-love, and blind opinion of true merit."

"I do not dislike the course this masque is taking," Prince Palador said.

Fourth, Grilla entered. She was wearing a rich gown with a great farthingale, aka hooped petticoat, a great ruff, a muff, a fan, and a coxcomb cap on her head. Her female clothing was out of fashion, and a coxcomb cap was a part of the costume of a professional Fool. She seemed to be portraying Foolish Pride, although Corax identified her form of Melancholy as Phrenitis, which is normally delirium accompanied by or caused by fever. Corax, however, will explain that pride is the ground — the foundation — of Phrenitis.

Grilla said, "Yes, indeed, and no, indeed. Isn't this fine! I ask you for your blessing, gaffer."

The word "gaffer" was a respectful title to use when addressing an elderly man.

She continued, "Here, here, here did he give me a shough — a long-haired lap-dog — and cut off its tail! Kiss, kiss, uncle, and there's a pum for daddy."

"Pum" was a lisped pronunciation of "plum."

Apparently, the gaffer was a sugar daddy.

Corax said to Prince Palador, "You find this noted there in the paper: It is called Phrenitis."

"True," Prince Palador said. "I see it."

"Pride is the ground of it," Corax said. "It reigns most often in women."

Fifth, Cuculus appeared, resembling a Bedlam madman. He was portraying a Hypochondriacal, someone suffering from ill health of the hypochondria, which are the regions of the upper chest under the ribs.

In character as a Hypochondriacal, Cuculus sang:

"They who will learn to drink a health in hell

"Must learn on earth to take tobacco well,

"To take tobacco well, to take tobacco well;

"For in hell they drink neither wine nor ale nor beer,

"But fire and smoke and stench, as we do here."

In character as Lycanthropia, Rhetias said, "I'll swoop in and sup you up."

In character as Hydrophobia, Pelias said, "You shall go immediately to execution."

In character as Phrenitis, Grilla said, "Fool, fool, fool! Catch me if you can."

In character, the Philosopher said, "Expel him from the house; he is a dunce."

In character as a Hypochondriacal, Cuculus sang:

"Listen! Didn't you hear a rumbling?

"The goblins are now a tumbling:

"I'll tear them, I'll sear them,

"I'll roar them, I'll gore them!

"Now, now, now! My brains are a jumbling —

"Boom! The gun's gone off."

Prince Palador said, "You name this type of Melancholy here Hypochondriacal?"

"Yes," Corax said. "It is a windy flatuous humor, stuffing the head, and thence derived to the animal parts. What causes it is being too over-curious, or suffering loss of goods or friends, or having excess of fear or of sorrow."

Sixth, a Sea-Nymph entered, portraying Wanton Melancholy. She was big-bellied — pregnant — and she danced as she sang:

"Good your honors,

"Pray your worships,

"Dear your beauties."

In character as a Hypochondriacal, Cuculus sang:

"Hang you!

"To lash your sides,

"To tame your hides,

"To scourge your prides;

"And bang [strike] you."

The Sea-Nymph sang:

"We're pretty and dainty, and I will begin:

"See, how they do jeer me, deride me, and grin.

"*Come sport me, come court me, your topsail advance,*
"*And let us conclude our delights in a dance!*"
All the actors sang:
"*A dance, a dance, a dance!*"
The actors began to dance.

Corax explained the character of the Sea-Nymph, "This is the Wanton Melancholy. Pregnant women, possessed with this strange fury, often have danced three days altogether without ceasing."

This behavior was called Saint Vitus' dance, but its modern name is Sydenham's chorea. The afflicted person suffered from rapid jerky movements that observers called a dance; those who were afflicted often sought help by visiting a shrine devoted to Saint Vitus.

Prince Palador said, "It is very strange, but heaven is full of miracles."

Once the dance was over, the masquers exited in couples.

Using the royal plural, Prince Palador said, "We are your debtor, Corax, for the gift of this masque, but the paper deceives us."

He pointed to a place in the paper and asked, "What is the meaning of this empty space?"

Corax said, "Only one kind of Melancholy is left untouched. The masque was not able to impersonate the image of that fancy, which is named Love-Melancholy.

"As an example of Love-Melancholy, let's say that this stranger here —"
He said to Parthenophill, "Young man, stand forth."
Parthenophill stepped forward.

Corax continued, "Let's say that this young man, entangled by the beauty of this lady, the great Thamasta, cherished in his heart the weight of hopes and fears.

"It would be impossible to depict his passions in such lively colors as his own actual experience could express."

"You are not modest, sir," Parthenophill said.
He meant that Corax was being offensive.

"Am I your mirth?" Thamasta asked. "Are you making fun of me?"

Ignoring them, Corax said, "Love is the tyrant of the heart. It darkens reason and confounds discretion. It is deaf to counsel, and it runs a headlong course to desperate madness.

"Oh, if your highness were just touched home and thoroughly with this — what shall I call it? — devil —"

Prince Palador interrupted, "Stop! Let no man henceforth name the word again."

The word was "Love-Melancholy."

Prince Palador looked closely at Parthenophill, who was supposed to be a stranger who had recently come to his court. It was strange, but he seemed to have seen him before — and not recently.

He said to Parthenophill, "Expect a time when it will be my pleasure to see you, youth."

He then said to all present, "It is late; go and rest!"

He exited.

Corax now knew that Prince Palador was suffering from Love-Melancholy.

He began, "My lords —"

Knowing what he was going to say, Sophronos said, "Enough. You are a perfect arts-man. You are skilled in medicine."

Corax said, "Panthers may hide their heads, but not change the skin."

Panthers were believed to hide their heads and attract prey through the pleasurable scent and appearance of their skin.

He continued, "And love pent never so close, yet will be seen."

Prince Palador had been hiding the love he felt, but such love, no matter how closely it is shut up and hidden, will eventually be revealed.

CHAPTER 4
— 4.1 —

Amethus and Menaphon talked together in a room in Thamasta's house. They were talking about Thamasta, who was Amethus' sister and Menaphon's beloved.

"Does she dote on a stranger?" Amethus asked.

"She courts him," Menaphon said, "and she pleads with and sues to him."

"Affectionately?" Amethus asked.

"Servilely," Menaphon said, "and, pardon me if I say, basely."

"Women, in their passions, like false fires, flash, to frighten our trembling senses, yet women in themselves contain neither light nor heat," Amethus said.

A "false fire" is the firing of a firearm in which there is a blank.

According to Amethus, the passions of women, including his sister, were an outward show with no substance.

He added, "My sister do this! She, whose pride did scorn all thoughts that were not busied on a crown, to fall so far beneath her fortunes now!

"You are my friend."

"What I confirm is truth," Menaphon said.

"Truth, Menaphon?" Amethus asked.

"If I thought that you were suspicious of my sincerity and plainness, then, sir ..."

"What then, sir?" Amethus prompted.

"I would then resolve that you were as changeable in vows of friendship as is Thamasta in her choice of love," Menaphon said. "That sin is double, running in the blood, which justifies another sin's being worse."

"Running in the blood" means "inherited," aka "running in families."

The double sin, in this case, is 1) Amethus' being changeable in vows of friendship 2) in order to justify the worse sin of Thamasta's being changeable in her choice of whom to love. She had made Menaphon her servant but then had chosen to love Parthenophill.

"My Menaphon, excuse me," Amethus said. "I grow wild, and I would not willingly believe the truth of my dishonor. She shall know how much I am a debtor to your noble goodness by checking — restraining — the contempt her poor desires have sunk her reputation in.

"Please tell me, friend, how did the youth receive my sister?"

"With a coldness as modest and as hopeless as the trust I did repose in him could wish or merit," Menaphon said.

Menaphon had been very angry at Parthenophill because the youth was Thamasta's choice of a man to love, but time had passed, and perhaps he had calmed down somewhat and now realized that Parthenophill had actually behaved correctly in his responses to Thamasta.

"I will esteem him dearly," Amethus said.

Thamasta and Kala entered the room.

Menaphon said to Amethus, "Sir, your sister."

Thamasta said to Menaphon, "Servant, I have employment for you."

She was still referring to Menaphon as her devoted servant, aka wooer.

"Listen, you!" Amethus said to Thamasta. "The mask of your ambition has fallen off. Your pride has stooped to such an abject lowness that you have now disclosed these things to be gossiped about: your nakedness in virtue, honors, shame —"

"You have turned satiric," Thamasta interrupted.

"All the flatteries of greatness have exposed you to contempt," Amethus said.

Self-indulgent highly born people can delude themselves by thinking that because of their greatness they need not follow society's rules and customs of morality.

"This is mere railing," Thamasta said.

"You have sold your birth for lust," Amethus said.

In Genesis 25:29-34, Esau sold his birthright to Jacob for a meal.

"Lust!" Thamasta said.

"Yes," Amethus said, "and at a dear expense you have purchased only the glories of a wanton."

"A wanton!" Thamasta said.

"Let repentance stop your mouth," Amethus said. "Learn to redeem your fault."

Kala whispered to Menaphon, "I hope that your tongue has not betrayed my honesty."

"Fear nothing," Menaphon whispered back.

Thamasta said, "If, Menaphon, I hitherto have striven to keep a wary guard about my reputation, and if I have used a woman's skill to sift the constancy of your protested love, then you cannot, in the justice of your judgment, impute to a coyness or neglect that which my discretion and your service aimed for noble purposes."

"Great mistress, no," Menaphon said. "I am instead quarrelling with my own ambition that dared to soar so high as to feed the hope of any least merit that I might have that might entitle my duty to a pension, tribute, or wages from your favors."

Amethus said, "And therefore, lady, please, observe him well. He henceforth covets plain equality. Endeavoring to rank his fortunes low, with some fit partner, whom, without presumption and without offence or danger, he may cherish, yes, and command, too, as a wife, a wife, a wife, my most great lady!"

Amethus was saying that Menaphon was lowering his sights. Instead of pursuing a highly born lady such as Thamasta, he now preferred to pursue someone lower born — but someone he would be comfortable making his wife.

Kala thought, *All will come out. Everyone will know the part I played in this.*

Thamasta said, "Now I perceive that the league of amity and friendship, which you two have long between you vowed and kept, is sacred and inviolable. Secrets of every nature are in common to you.

"I have trespassed, and I have been faulty. Let not too rude a censure doom me guilty, or judge that my error is willful without pardon."

"Gracious and virtuous mistress!" Menaphon said.

Menaphon was happy with Thamasta's apology.

Amethus, however, said, "It's a trick. There is no trust in female cunning, friend. Let her first purge her past follies, and clear the wrong done to her honor, by some sure and apparent evidence of her constancy and loyalty, or we will not believe these childish plots, weak excuses, and unconvincing apologies. As you respect my friendship, don't listen to what Thamasta will say in reply. Think about what I have said!"

Menaphon said to Thamasta, "Please, love your reputation."

Amethus and Menaphon exited.

"Gone!" Thamasta said. "I am surely awake.

"Kala, I find that you have not been so trusty as the duty you owed to me required."

"Haven't I?" Kala said. "I protest that I have been, madam."

Thamasta said, "No matter what the truth of that is, I'm paid in my own coin.

"There is something I must do, and speedily. So!

"Seek and find Cuculus. Tell him to come to me instantly."

"That gargoyle!" Kala said. "The trim old youth shall wait on you."

Thamasta said, "Wounds may be mortal, which are wounds indeed, but no wound's deadly until our honors bleed."

Rhetias and Corax talked together in a room in the castle.

Rhetias said, "You are an excellent fellow. Diabolo — Devil! Oh, these lousy close-stool empirics — toilet-quality quacks — who will undertake all cures, yet don't know the causes of any disease! They are doctors for dogs! By the four elements — fire, air, earth, and water — I honor you; I could find in my heart the desire to turn knave and be your flatterer."

Corax said, "Sirrah, it is a pity you have not been a scholar. You are honest, blunt, and rude enough, I say in conscience.

"But as for your lord — Meleander — now, I have put him to it."

Rhetias said, "He chafes hugely, fumes like a stew-pot. Hasn't he monstrously been overrun with frenzy?"

"Rhetias, it is not a madness, but his sorrow's close-gripping grief and anguish of the soul that torture him. He carries hell on earth within his bosom. It was a prince's tyranny that caused his distraction, and another prince's sweetness must qualify that tempest of his mind."

The tyrannous prince was Agenor, Prince Palador's father, and the sweet prince is Palador.

Rhetias said, "Corax, to praise your art would be like assuring the misbelieving world that the sun shines when it is in the full meridian — high noon — of its beauty. No cloud of black detraction can eclipse the light of your rare and splendid knowledge.

"Henceforth, I will cast off all poor disguises that play in rudeness. I will stop being churlish and cynical.

"Call me your servant. For the present, I only wish a happy blessing to your labors. May Heaven crown your undertakings!

"Believe me, before many hours can pass, at our next meeting, the bonds my duty owes shall be fully cancelled."

He may have been saying that he expected Corax' efforts to cure Meleander would be successful before much longer.

"Farewell," Corax said.

Rhetias exited.

Corax said about Rhetias, "He is a shrewd-brained whoreson; there is pith — substance — in his untoward — perverse — plainness."

He was using the word "whoreson" as a term of rough affection.

Rhetias and Corax were similar in that underneath their hard exteriors lay soft interiors.

Trollio, who was wearing a helmet, entered the room.

Corax asked, "Now, what is the news?"

"Worshipful Master Doctor, I have a great deal of I cannot tell what to say to you," Trollio said. "My lord Meleander thunders; every word that comes out of his mouth roars like a cannon; the house shook once; and my young lady Cleophila dares not be seen."

"We will roar with him, Trollio, if he roars," Corax said.

"Meleander has got a great poleaxe in his hand, and fences it up and down the house, as if he were to make room for the pageants," Trollio said.

Armed city officials would clear the streets to make room when there was a procession.

He continued, "I have provided myself with a helmet out of fear of a clap on the coxcomb."

A coxcomb is a head.

Corax said, "I won't need a helmet; here's my cap. Thus I will pull it down, and thus I will outstare him."

Trollio thought, *The physician has become as mad as my lord.*

He said out loud, "Oh, splendid! You are a man of worship — you are a man to be honored."

"Let him come, Trollio," Corax said. "I will firk his trangdido — strike his backside — and bounce and bounce and bluster in metal, honest Trollio."

He was humorously saying that he would defeat Meleander in a fight. Of course, one way to defeat someone is through the use of one's wits.

Trollio thought, *He boasts like a tinker and struts like a juggler.*

Outside the room, Meleander called, "So-ho! So-ho!"

This was a hunting cry.

"There, there, there!" Trollio said. "Look to your right worshipful — look to yourself."

Brandishing a poleaxe, Meleander entered the room.

Meleander shouted, "Show me the dog whose triple-throated noise has roused a lion from his uncouth den to tear the cur into pieces."

The dog with the triple throat is the three-headed Cerberus, a guard dog of the Land of the Dead. The lion is Hercules, whose first labor was to slay the Nemean Lion, whose hide could not be pierced by any ordinary weapons. Hercules strangled the Nemean Lion, and then he used its claws to skin it. Thereafter, he wore its hide. One of Hercules' famous labors was to drag Cerberus out of the Land of the Dead.

Corax pulled his cap down, partially hiding his face, turned to Meleander, and said, "Restrain your paws, courageous beast; else, look, the Gorgon's skull, which shall transform you to that restless stone which Sisyphus rolls up against the hill, whence, it tumbling down again, its weight shall crush your bones and puff you into air."

According to mythology, anyone who saw a Gorgon, a female monster with snakes for hair, was turned to stone.

Sisyphus' punishment in the Land of the Dead was meaningless work. He was assigned the task of rolling a heavy stone up a high hill, but every time he neared the top, he lost control of the stone and it rolled down again.

"Hold, hold your conquering breath," Meleander said. "It is far stronger than gunpowder and garlic. If the Fates have spun my thread, and my spent ball of thread and life is now untwisted, let us part like friends."

The three Fates commanded the pulse of life; they controlled human life. Clotho spun the thread of life. Lachesis measured the thread of life, determining how long a person lived. Atropos cut the thread of life; when the thread was cut, the person died.

Meleander ordered, "Lay up my weapon, Trollio, and be gone."

"Yes, sir, with all my heart," Trollio said, taking the poleax from him.

Meleander said, "This friend and I will walk, and we will gabble wisely."

Trollio exited with the poleax.

Corax said, "I agree with your proposal."

He pulled his cap back on top of his head.

Meleander said, "So politicians thrive, who, with their crabbed faces and sly tricks, legerdemain, bows, cringes, formal beards, crisped hairs, and ceremonial cheats, do wriggle in their heads first, like a fox, to rooms of state, and then the whole body follows."

Corax said, "Then they fill lordships, steal women's hearts, and with them and theirs the world runs round; yet these are square — unimpeachable — men still."

"There are none poor but such as engross and monopolize offices," Meleander said.

"There are none wise but the unthrifty, bankrupts, beggars, and rascals," Corax said.

"The hangman is a splendid physician," Meleander said.

Corax thought, *That's not so good.*

He then said out loud, "What you say shall be granted."

Meleander said, "All the busy talk and gossip of drugs and minerals and medicinal herbs, bloodlettings, vomits, purges, or whatever else is conjured up by men of art and skill, to gull liege-people, and rear golden piles, are trash to a strong well-wrought halter; there on the gibbet the gout, the kidney stone, yes, and the melancholy devil, are cured in less time than a pair of minutes.

"Build me a gallows in this very plot, and I'll dispatch your business."

Death cures all illnesses; kill a person who has cancer, and the cancer dies.

Corax said, "Fix the knot right under the left ear."

"Sirrah, make yourself ready," Meleander said.

"Yet do not be too sudden," Corax said. "Grant me permission to give a farewell to a creature long absented from me. It is a daughter, sir, snatched from me in her youth; she is a handsome girl. She comes to ask a blessing."

"Please tell me," Meleander said, "where is she? I cannot see her yet."

"She makes more haste in her quick prayers than her trembling steps, which many griefs have weakened," Corax said.

"Cruel man!" Meleander said. "How can you rip a heart that's cleft already with injuries of time?

"While I am frantic, while throngs of rude divisions huddle on and disorder my brains, keeping them from peace and sleep, so long I am insensible of cares.

"As balls of wildfire may be safely touched, not violently sundered and thrown up, so my distempered thoughts rest in their rage, not hurried in the air of repetition, or memory of my misfortunes past.

"Then my griefs are struck home, when they're reclaimed to their own pity of themselves.

"Proceed. What of your daughter now?"

"I cannot tell you," Corax said. "It is now out of my head again; my brains are crazy. I have scarcely slept one sound sleep these past twelve months."

"It's a pity, poor man!" Meleander said. "Can you imagine you can prosper in the task you take in hand by practicing a cure upon my weakness, and yet be no physician for yourself?

"Go, go, turn over all your books once more, and learn to thrive in modesty; for impudence least becomes a scholar.

"You are a fool, a kind of learned fool."

"I confess that that is true," Corax said.

Meleander said, "If you can stay awake with me, forget to eat, renounce the thought of greatness, tread on fate, sigh out a lamentable tale of things done long ago, and ill done, and, when sighs are wearied, gather together what grief remains behind with weeping eyes, and hearts that bleed to death, then you shall be a companion fit for me, and we will sit together, like true friends, and never be separated.

"With what greediness do I hug my afflictions! There's no mirth that is not truly seasoned with some madness. As, for example —"

He exited hastily.

"What new crotchet will he have next?" Corax asked himself. "There is so much sense in this wild distraction that I am almost out of my wits, too, to see and hear him. A few more hours spent here would turn me fantastically foolish like an ape, if not frantic."

Meleander returned with his daughter Cleophila.

He said, "In all the books you have consulted, you man of knowledge, have you met with any rarity worthy your contemplation like this woman?

"The model of the heavens, the earth, the waters, the harmony and sweet consent of times, are not of such an excellence, in form of their creation, as the infinite wonder that dwells within the compass of this face.

"And yet I tell you, scholar, that under this well-ordered sign is lodged such an obedience as will hereafter, in another age, strike all comparison into a silence."

He was saying that Cleophila was a metaphorical astrological sign signifying obedience.

Meleander continued, "She had a sister, too, named Eroclea, but as for her, if I were given to talk, I could describe a pretty piece of goodness — let that pass. We must be wise sometimes.

"What do you want with her?"

"I with her!" Corax said. "Nothing, by your leave, sir, I. It is not my profession."

Corax was not a pimp or a whoremonger.

"You are saucy," Meleander said, "and as I take it, scurvy in your sauciness, to use no more respect."

He said to his daughter, "Good soul, be patient. We are a pair of things that the world laughs at. Yet be content, Cleophila; those clouds, which bar the sun from shining on our miseries, will never be chased off until I am dead, and then some charitable soul will take you and protect you.

"I am hastening on to the end of my life. The time of my upcoming death cannot be long."

"I beg you, sir," Cleophila said to her father, "as you love your health and as you respect my safety, don't let passion overrule you."

"It shall not," Meleander replied. "I am friends with all the world.

"Get me some wine; to witness that I will be an absolute good fellow, I will drink with you."

Corax whispered to Cleophila, "Have you prepared his cup?"

She whispered back, "It is ready."

Cuculus and Grilla entered the room.

"By your leave, gallants," Cuculus said, "I come to speak with a young lady, as they say, the old Trojan's daughter of the house."

"Trojan" is a slang word for a boon companion.

"What is your business with my lady-daughter, tosspot?" Meleander asked.

A tosspot is a drunkard.

Grilla said, "Tosspot! Oh, base! Tosspot!"

"Quiet!" Cuculus said to her. "Don't you see what condition he is in?"

He said to Meleander, "I would do my own commendations to her; that's all."

"Do that," Meleander replied.

He then said to Corax, "Come, my Genius, we will quaff in wine until we grow wise."

A Genius is a protective spirit, a guardian angel.

"True nectar is divine," Corax said.

Meleander and Corax exited.

"Good!" Cuculus said. "I am glad he is gone."

He said to Grilla, "Page, walk to the side and give us some privacy."

He then said to Cleophila, "Sweet beauty, I am sent as an ambassador from the mistress of my thoughts — Thamasta — to you, the mistress of my desires."

"I see, sir," Cleophila said. "Please, be brief."

Cuculus said, "So that you may know I am not, as they say, an animal, which is, as they say, a kind of simpleton, which is, as the learned term it, an ass, a puppy, a widgeon, a dolt, a noddy, a —"

"As you please," Cleophila interrupted.

"Pardon me for that," Cuculus said. "It shall be as you please indeed. Truly, I love to be courtly and in fashion."

"Well, get to your embassy," Cleophila said. "What is it, and from whom is it?"

"Indeed, 'what' is more than I know; for to know what's what is to know what's what and for what's what, but these are foolish figures of speech and to little purpose," Cuculus said.

"From whom, then, are you sent?" Cleophila asked.

"There you come to me again," Cuculus said. "Oh, to be in the favor of great ladies is as much to say as to be great in ladies' favors."

Ladies' favors can include sex.

"Good day to you!" Cleophila said. "I can stay no longer."

Cuculus said, "By this light" — this meant either "By the sun's light" or "By God's light" — "I swear that you must stay, for now I come to the point. The most excellent, most wise, most dainty, precious, loving, kind, sweet, intolerably fair Lady Thamasta commends to your little hands this letter of importance. With your permission, let me first kiss the letter, and then deliver it according to fashion to your own proper beauty."

He kissed the letter and then handed it to her.

"To me, from Thamasta?" Cleophila said. "That is strange! I dare to read it."

She began to read the letter.

"Good," Cuculus said. "Oh, I wish that I had not resolved to live a single life! Here's temptation, able to conjure up a spirit with a witness."

What was being conjured up was his spirited penis.

"With a witness" means "emphatically" or "with a vengeance."

He then thought, *So! So! She has read the letter.*

"Is it possible?" Cleophila said. "Heaven, you are great and bountiful."

Thamasta had received and read the letter that Parthenophill, who had revealed to her that he was really a she, had written for her. In that letter, Parthenophill had revealed another secret that Thamasta was now sharing with Cleophila.

Cleophila then said to Cuculus, "Sir, I much thank you for your pains, and let my love, duty, service be remembered to the Princess Thamasta."

"They shall, madam," Cuculus said.

He verbally stumbled over the word "madam," which came out like "mad-dame."

Cleophila said, "When we are quite bereft of hopes or helps, our humble prayers have entrance into heaven."

"That's my opinion clearly and without doubt," Cuculus said.

Aretus and Sophronos spoke together in a room in the palace.

"The prince is thoroughly moved," Aretus said. "He is very emotional."

"I have never seen him so much distempered and out of balance," Sophronos said.

"Who could this young man be?" Aretus asked, referring to Parthenophill. "Or to where can he have been conveyed?"

"To me it is a mystery," Sophronos said. "I don't understand it."

"Nor do I," Aretus said.

Prince Palador, Amethus, and Pelias entered the room.

Prince Palador said, "All of you have consented to work upon the softness of my nature, but take heed. Although I can sleep in silence, and look on the mockery you make of my dull patience, yet you shall know, the best of you, that in me there is a masculine spirit, a stirring spirit, which, when it is provoked, shall, like a bearded comet — a comet with a tail — make you stare with fascination, and it shall threaten horror."

In this society, comets were regarded as malevolent omens.

Pelias began, "Good sir —"

"Good sir!" Prince Palador interrupted. "It is not your active wit or language, nor your grave politic wisdoms, lords, that shall dare to checkmate and control my just commands."

Menaphon entered the room.

Prince Palador asked, "Where is the youth, your friend? Has he been found yet?"

"He is not to be heard of," Menaphon said.

Prince Palador said, "Fly, then, to the desert, where you first encountered this fantastic figure, this airy apparition — come no more into my sight!

"All of you, get away from me. He who stays is not my friend."

Amethus said, "It is strange."

Aretus and Sophronos said, "We must obey."

Everyone except Prince Palador exited.

Alone, he said to himself, "Some angry power cheats with rare delusions my credulous sense; the very soul of reason is troubled in me.

"Corax the physician presented a strange masque about melancholy to me. Seeing the masque puzzled my understanding, but the boy Parthenophill —"

He stopped talking because Rhetias was entering the room.

Prince Palador said, "Rhetias, you are acquainted with my griefs. Parthenophill is lost, and I want to see him, for he is similar to something I remember a great while since, a long, long time ago."

"I have been diligent, sir, to pry into every corner to discover him, but I cannot find him," Rhetias said. "There is some trick involved, I am confident."

"True," Prince Palador said. "There is some practice, sleight, or plot."

Rhetias said, "I have apprehended a fair wench in an odd private lodging in the city, as like the youth Parthenophill in the face as can by possibility be discerned."

"What, Rhetias!" Prince Palador said.

"If it is not Parthenophill wearing long petticoats, it is a spirit in his likeness. I can get no answer from her to my questions; you shall see her."

"This is the young man — Parthenophill — in disguise, I swear upon my life, so he can steal out of the land."

"I'll send him to you," Rhetias said.

"Do, do, my Rhetias," Prince Palador said.

Rhetias exited.

Alone, Prince Palador said to himself, "As there is by nature in everything created contrariety, so likewise is there unity and league between them in their kind."

An example of this is male and female. They are opposites, but they can unite.

Prince Palador continued, "But man, the compendium of all perfection, which the workmanship of heaven has modeled, in himself contains passions of several qualities."

Humankind, which is more perfect than plants and animals, is capable of many different emotions.

Wearing women's clothing, Parthenophill entered the room and stood behind Prince Palador.

Parthenophill was either pretending to be Eroclea — or "he" really was Eroclea and had spent the last few years in disguise as a young man.

Prince Palador continued, "The music of man's fair composition best accords when it is in consort, not in single strains."

A man needs a wife who is in harmony with him.

He continued, "My heart has been untuned these many months, lacking and wanting her — Eroclea's — presence, in whose equal love my heart's true harmony consisted.

"Living here, we all are heaven's bounty, but we are also fortune's exercise. Our existence on Earth is a gift from Heaven, but we are subjects to Lady Fortune."

Parthenophill, dressed in women's clothing, said, "Minutes are numbered by the fall of sands, as by an hourglass; the span of time passes and wastes us to our graves, and we look at and reflect on the passage of time.

"An age of pleasures, reveled out, comes home at last, and ends in sorrow, but the life, weary of riot, numbers every sand, wailing in sighs, until the last teardrop drips down.

"And so we conclude the calamity of life with eternal rest."

"What echo yields a voice to my complaints?" Prince Palador asked. "Can I be nowhere private?"

Parthenophill, dressed in women's clothing, came forward, knelt, and said, "Let the substance as suddenly be hurried from your eyes as the vain sound can pass from your ear, if no impression of a troth vowed yours does retain a constant memory."

The substance was Parthenophill, and the sound was Parthenophill's voice.

The troth was Prince Palador's and Eroclea's vow to be married.

"Stand up," Prince Palador ordered.

Parthenophill, dressed in women's clothing, stood up.

Prince Palador looked at Parthenophill, dressed in women's clothing. He saw a resemblance to Eroclea, but he was not convinced that Parthenophill was Eroclea. Instead, Parthenophill seemed like a counterfeit coin that had been stamped with a portrait of a notable figure.

Prince Palador said, "It is not the figure stamped upon your cheeks, the cozenage of your beauty, grace, or tongue that can draw from me a secret that has been the only jewel of my speechless thoughts."

Parthenophill, dressed in women's clothing, said, "I am so worn away with fears and sorrows, so wintered with the tempests of affliction, that the bright sun of your life-quickening presence has scarcely one beam of force to warm again that spring of cheerful comfort, which youth once clothed in fresh looks."

"Cunning impostor!" Prince Palador said. "Untruth has made you subtle in your trade.

"Perhaps a neighboring state has seduced a free-born resolution to attempt some bolder act of treachery by cutting my weary days off.

"For that reason, you cruel-mercy, you have assumed a shape that would make treason a piety, guilt pardonable, and bloodshed as holy as the sacrifice of peace!"

Parthenophill, dressed in women's clothing, said, "The incense of my love-desires is burning upon an altar of more constant proof.

"Sir, oh, sir, turn me back into the world. Command me to forget my name, my birth, my father's sadness, and my death while I am alive, if all remembrance of my faith has found a burial without pity in your scorn!"

Parthenophill, dressed in women's clothing, was saying that Parthenophill — that is, Eroclea — had been faithful to Prince Palador.

But was Parthenophill really Eroclea?

"My scorn, disdainful boy, shall soon unweave the web that your art has twisted," Prince Palador said. "Cast your shape off, disrobe the mantle of a feigned sex, and so I may be gentle.

"As you now are, there's witchcraft in your language, in your face, in your demeanors.

"Turn, turn away from me, please, for my belief is armed else.

"Yet, fair subtlety, before we part, for part we must, tell me the truth.

"Tell me your country."

"Cyprus," Parthenophill, dressed in women's clothing, answered.

"Ha!" Prince Palador said. "Who is your father?"

"Meleander," Parthenophill, dressed in women's clothing, answered.

"Do you have a name?" Prince Palador asked.

"I have a name of misery: I am the unfortunate Eroclea," Parthenophill, dressed in women's clothing, answered.

"There is danger in this seducing counterfeit," Prince Palador said. "Great goodness, have honesty and virtue left the time?

"Have we become so impious that to tread the path of impudence is law and justice?

"You mask of a beauty forever sacred, tell me your name."

Parthenophill, dressed in women's clothing, answered, "While I was lost to memory, 'Parthenophill' did shroud my shame in change of sundry rare misfortunes, but, since now I have, before I die, returned to claim a funeral train to my grave, I must not blush to let Prince Palador, if I offend, know that when he judges and sentences me, that he judges and sentences Eroclea. I am Eroclea — that woeful maid."

"Don't join too fast your penance with the story of my sufferings," Prince Palador said. "So simplicity dwelt with virgin truth, so martyrdom and holiness are twins, as innocence and sweetness are on your tongue.

"But let me by degrees collect my senses: I may abuse my trust by mistakenly trusting you.

"Tell me, what air have you perfumed, since tyranny first ravished the contract of our hearts?"

In other words, where has Eroclea been since Prince Palador's tyrant father interfered with their happiness?

Parthenophill, dressed in women's clothing, answered, "Dear sir, in Athens I have been buried."

In other words, Eroclea had been hidden and in disguise in Athens.

"Buried!" Prince Palador said. "Right; you have been metaphorically buried in Athens as I have been metaphorically buried in Cyprus.

"Come, here's a test and trial. If you really are Eroclea, in my bosom I can find you."

He was wearing Eroclea's miniature portrait around his neck; earlier, he had shown the portrait to Rhetias.

"As I can find Prince Palador in my bosom," Parthenophill, dressed in women's clothing, answered, revealing a miniature portrait of Prince Palador. Like the prince's portrait of Eroclea, this portrait was designed to hang around the neck.

Parthenophill, dressed in women's clothing, said, "This gift his bounty blessed me with — it is the only medicine my solitary cares have hourly taken to keep me from despair."

Seeing the miniature portrait, a gift from his own hands, Prince Palador knew with no doubt that Parthenophill, standing before him and dressed in women's clothing, was no boy. Parthenophill was, with absolutely no doubt, Eroclea.

From here on, this book refers to Parthenophill by his — her — real name: Eroclea.

Prince Palador said to the now revealed Eroclea, "We are but fools to trifle in disputes, or vainly struggle with that eternal mercy which protects us.

"Come home, home to my heart, you banished peace!

"My ecstasy of joys would speak in passion, except that I would not lose that part of man — the rational part — which is reserved to entertain content.

"Eroclea, I am yours. Oh, let me seize you as my inheritance! Hymen, the god of marriage, shall now set all his torches burning, to give light throughout this land, new-settled in your welcome."

The now revealed Eroclea said, "You are still gracious, sir. How I have lived, by what means been conveyed, by what preserved, and by what returned, Rhetias, my trusty servant, directed by the wisdom of my uncle, the good Sophronos, can inform you in complete detail."

"Enough," Prince Palador said. "Instead of music, every night, to make our sleeps delightful, you shall close our weary eyes with some part of your story."

"Oh, but my father!" the now revealed Eroclea said.

"Don't worry," Prince Palador said. "His beholding Eroclea — you — and knowing that she is — you are — safe will make him young again: It shall be our first task.

"Blush, sensual follies, which are not guarded with chastely pure thoughts. There is no faith in lust, but baits of arts — clever, tricky enticements.

"It is virtuous love that keeps clear contracted hearts."

CHAPTER 5

— 5.1 —

Corax and Cleophila talked together in a room in the castle.

"It is well, it is well," Corax said. "The hour is at hand that must conclude the business — the business that no skill could all this while make ripe for wished content.

"Oh, lady, in the turmoils of our lives, men are like politic states, or troubled seas, tossed up and down with several storms and tempests, change and variety of wrecks and fortunes, until laboring to the havens of our homes, we struggle for the calm that crowns our ends."

"May heaven bless us with a happy end!" Cleophila said.

"It is well said," Corax said. "The old man still sleeps soundly."

"May soft dreams play in his fancy, so that when he awakes, with comfort he may, by degrees, digest the present blessings in a moderate joy!" Cleophila said.

"I drugged his cup for that purpose," Corax said. "He never stirred while at the barber's or at the tailor's. He will laugh at his own metamorphosis, and wonder."

While sleeping a drugged sleep, Meleander had been taken to a barber's for a haircut and beard trimming and to a tailor's for new, fresh clothing.

Corax continued, "We must be watchful. Does the coach stand ready?"

The coach was a small one that would be used to transport Meleander while he was sleeping.

"All has been arranged as you commanded," Cleophila said.

Trollio ran into the room.

Cleophila asked, "What's your haste for?"

"A brace of important women, ushered by the young old ape with his she-clog at his bum, have entered the castle," Trollio said.

The young old ape with his she-clog at his bum was Cuculus, who was with Grilla.

Trollio then asked, "Shall they come in?"

"By all means," Corax said. "The time is precious now."

He said to Cleophila, "Lady, be quick and careful."

He then said, "Follow me, Trollio."

Trollio said, "I owe all sir-reverence to your right worshipfulness."

The word combination "sir-reverence" meant 1) "saving your reverence," aka "with all due respect," and 2) "human excrement."

Corax and Trollio exited.

Alone, Cleophila said to herself, "So many fears and so many joys encounter my doubtful expectations that I waver between the answer to my hopes and my obedience to my father: It is not — oh, my fate! — the apprehension of a timely blessing in pleasures that shakes my weakness, but the danger of a mistaken duty that confines the limits of my reason."

Cleophila was hoping for "a timely blessing in pleasures": a marriage to Amethus. The "mistaken duty" was to her father: She had been taking care of him out of a proper sense of familial duty, but if things worked out in the near future, she would not need to take such care of him. Without that necessity, it would be a mistake to take care of him at the expense of her happiness in a good marriage. Uncertainty about future events made rational thought difficult. Would her father truly recover from his illness?

She continued, "Let me live, virtue, to you as chaste as truth is to time!"

She wished to be virtuous and do the right thing by her father, but she also wished to be happily married without sacrificing the proper familial duty of taking care of her father when he truly needed such help.

Thamasta entered the room while saying to someone outside, "Wait here until I call for you."

Was Kala the someone outside? Would the comic character Trollio regard her as a big woman?

She then said, "My sweet Cleophila!"

Cleophila began, "Great princess —"

Thamasta interrupted, "I bring peace, and I wish to ask for a pardon for my neglect of all those noble virtues that your mind and duty are appareled with.

"I have deserved ill from you, and I must say that you are too gentle if you can forget what I have done to deserve ill from you."

"You have not wronged me," Cleophila said, "for, indeed, acquaintance with my sorrows and my fortune were grown to such familiarity that it was an impudence, more than presumption, to wish that so great a lady as you are would lose affection on my uncle's son: Menaphon.

"But that your brother, equal to you in your blood and rank, should stoop to such a lowness as to love a castaway, a poor despised maiden — me — for me only to hope for that was almost a sin.

"Yet, truly, I never tempted him."

Thamasta replied, "Chide not the grossness of my trespass, lovely sweetness, in such humble language. I have smarted already in the wounds my pride has made upon your sufferings. Henceforth, it lies in you to bring about my happiness."

"Call any service of mine a debt," Cleophila said, "for such it is. The letter you recently sent me, in the blest contents it made me privy to, has abundantly cleared and gotten rid of every suspicion of your grace or goodness."

Thamasta said, "Let me embrace you with a sister's love — a sister's love, Cleophila — for should Amethus, my brother, henceforth study to forget the vows of love that he has made you, I would forever plead to him to give you what your merits deserve."

Thamasta was hoping that she and Cleophila would soon become sisters-in-law.

Outside the room, Amethus and Menaphon shouted, "We must have entrance."

"Must!" Thamasta said. "Who are they who say 'must'? You are unmannerly."

Amethus and Menaphon entered the room.

Thamasta said, "Brother, is it you? And you, too, sir?"

Her brother, Amethus, said to her, "Your ladyship has had a time of scolding to your humor."

Amethus then asked her, "Does the storm hold still?"

Cleophila answered for Thamasta, "Never has a shower more seasonably gentle fallen on the barren parched thirsty earth than showers of courtesy have from this princess been distilled on me, to make my growth in the quiet of my mind secure and lasting."

Thamasta said, "You may both believe that I was not uncivil."

"Pish!" Amethus said, still worried that his sister had been uncivil to Cleophila. "I know her — Thamasta's — spirit and her — Thamasta's — envy."

"Now, by my truth, sir," Cleophila said, "please believe me. I am not accustomed to swear.

"The virtuous princess has in words and carriage been kind, so over-kind, that I blush I am not rich enough in giving thanks sufficient for her unequaled bounty."

She then said to Menaphon, "My good cousin, I have a request to make to you."

"It shall be granted," Menaphon replied.

Cleophila said, "I request that no time, no persuasion, no respects of jealousies, past, present, or hereafter by any possibility to be conceived, may draw you from that sincerity and pureness of love that you have often professed to this great worthy lady: Thamasta. She deserves a duty more than what the ties of marriage can claim or warrant. Be forever hers, as she is yours, and may heaven increase your comforts!"

She wanted Menaphon and Thamasta to marry.

Amethus said, "Cleophila has played the churchman's part; I'll not forbid the banns."

He had no objection to his sister's marrying Menaphon. The banns were a proclamation of marriage.

"Do you agree to marry me?" Menaphon asked Thamasta.

She replied, "I have one task to take care of first, which is of concern to me."

She said to Amethus, "Brother, be not more cruel than this lady: Cleophila. She has forgiven my follies, and so may you. Her youth, beauty, innocence, discretion, without the additions of estate or birth, are dower enough for a prince, indeed. You loved her, for surely you swore you did. Or else, if you did not, then fix your heart on her, and know that if you now miss this heaven on earth, you cannot find in any other choice anything but a hell."

"The ladies are turned lawyers," Amethus said, "and they plead handsomely their clients' cases. I'm an easy judge; and so shall you be, Menaphon.

"I give you my sister to be your wife. She will be a good wife, friend."

Menaphon asked, "Lady, will you confirm the gift?"

"The errors of my mistaken judgment being lost to your remembrance, I shall always strive in my obedience to deserve your pity," Thamasta said.

"You deserve my love, my care, my all!" Menaphon said.

"What remains for me to do?" Amethus said. "I'm still a bachelor."

He then asked Cleophila, "Sweet maiden, tell me, may I yet call you mine?"

"My Lord Amethus, blame not my plain-spokenness," Cleophila replied. "I am young and innocent, and I have not any power to dispose my own will without permission from my father. Once my father's permission is acquired, I am yours."

"This answer satisfies me," Amethus said.

Cuculus, Pelias, and Trollio entered the room, dragging behind them Grilla.

"Revenge!" Cuculus shouted. "I must have revenge! I will have revenge, bitter and abominable revenge! I will have revenge! This unfashionable mongrel, this linsey-woolsey of mortality by this hand, mistress, this she-rogue is drunk, and clapperclawed — scratched and beat — me, without any respect for my person or good garments."

Literally, "linsey-woolsey" is cloth made of flax and wool; figuratively, it is neither one thing nor another. This is an appropriate description of Grilla, who was a boy dressed in girl's clothing.

Cuculus continued, "Why don't you speak, gentlemen?"

"Some certain blows have passed, if it like your highness, " Pelias said.

"Some few knocks of friendship, some love-toys, some cuffs in kindness, or so," Trollio said.

"I'll turn him away," Grilla said. "He shall be my master no longer."

"Is this your she-page, Cuculus?" Menaphon said. "This is a boy, surely."

"A boy, an arrant boy in long petticoats," Cuculus said.

"Grilla has mauled Cuculus' nose so that it is as big as a great codpiece," Trollio said.

A codpiece was a pouch that covered a man's genitals.

Cuculus said to Grilla, "Oh, you cock-vermin of iniquity!"

Thamasta ordered, "Pelias, take away from here the wag — Grilla — and discipline him for what he has done."

She then said to Cuculus, "And for your part, servant, I'll entreat Prince Palador to grant you some fit place about his wardrobe."

She would find him a position close to the prince.

These days some such positions may not be regarded as desirable. The Groom of the Stool assisted kings such as King Henry VIII with their defecations, supplying cleaning materials and removing the waste. An old or infirm king might even need help wiping his own bottom.

Cuculus said, "I always dream of good luck after I suffer a bloody nose.

"I horribly thank your ladyship.

"While I'm in office, the former fashion of having male pages shall again become fashionable, and tailors shall be men.

"Come, Trollio, help to wash my face, please."

"Yes, and to scour it, too," Trollio said.

One meaning of scour is to clear out a channel by removing dirt. Trollio may have been saying that Cuculus needed to blow his nose.

Cuculus, Trollio, Pelias, and Grilla exited.

Corax and Rhetias entered the room after the others exited.

Rhetias said, "The prince and princess — Palador and Eroclea — are at hand; stop your amorous dialogues."

"Most honored lady, henceforth forbear your sadness," he said to Cleophila. "Are you ready to put into effect your instructions?"

"I have studied my part with care, and I will perform it, Rhetias, with all the skill I can," Cleophila replied.

"I'll give my word that she will do what she says she will do," Corax said.

Trumpets sounded, and Prince Palador, Sophronos, Aretus, and Eroclea entered the room.

Prince Palador said, "Thus princes should be encircled, with a guard of truly noble friends and watchful subjects.

"Oh, Rhetias, you are a just man; the youth you told me about who lived at Athens has returned at last to her own fortunes and her contracted love."

The contracted love was Prince Palador's and Eroclea's engagement to be married.

Rhetias said, "My knowledge made me sure of my report, sir."

Prince Palador said, "Eroclea, clear away your fears. When the sun shines, clouds must not dare to muster in the sky, nor shall they here."

Cleophila and Amethus knelt.

"Why do they kneel?" Prince Palador asked.

He then said, "Stand up. The day and place are privileged."

On this day of rejoicing, Prince Palador was setting aside normal forms of courtly courtesy.

Sophronos said, "Your presence, great sir, makes every room a holy place: a sanctuary."

Amethus stood up.

Prince Palador said, "Why does this young virgin — Cleophila — kneel in duty to us? Rise."

Eroclea said, "It is I who must raise her."

She held Cleophila's hand and helped her stand up.

Eroclea said, "Forgive me, sister. I have been too private in hiding from your knowledge any secret that should have been in common between our souls, but I was ruled by counsel."

Sophronos, her uncle, had advised her about what she should do.

Weeping, Cleophila said, "I hope you cannot blame me for showing myself to be a girl, sister, and revealing my joy in too soft a passion before all these people."

She and Eroclea, who was also weeping, hugged each other.

Prince Palador said, "We must part the sudden meeting of these two fair rivulets with the island of our arms."

He stood between them with his arms around them.

He then said, "Cleophila, the custom of your piety has built, even to your younger years, a monument of memorable fame. Some great reward must wait on your desert."

Sophronos said to Cleophila, "The prince speaks to you, niece."

Corax said, "Chat softly, please; let us set about our business.

"The good old man awakes.

"My lord, withdraw.

"Rhetias, let's set the coach here."

Prince Palador said, "Let's leave, then!"

They left to set about their duties.

Soft music played.

Corax and Rhetias brought into the room a coach in which Meleander was sleeping. We might prefer to call the coach a wheelchair that could recline. Meleander's hair and beard had been trimmed, and he was wearing new clothing.

While they brought in the coach and set it down, a boy sang:

"*Fly hence, shadows that do keep*

"*Watchful sorrows charmed in sleep!*

"*Though the eyes be overtaken,*

"*Yet the heart does ever [always] waken*

"*Thoughts, chained up in busy snares*

"*Of continual woes and cares:*

"*Love and griefs are so expressed*

"*As they rather sigh than rest.*

"*Fly hence, shadows, that do keep*

"*Watchful sorrows charmed in sleep!*"

Meleander woke up and said, "Where am I? Ha! What sounds are these? It is daytime, surely.

"Oh, I have slept, in all probability; it is but the foolery of some beguiling dream. So! So! I will not trouble the play of my delighted fancy, but dream my dream out."

He had been having a good dream.

Corax said, "Good morning to your lordship! You took a jolly nap, and slept soundly."

"Go away, beast!" Meleander said. "Let me alone."

He wanted to return to his good dream.

"Oh, by your leave, sir," Corax said, "I must be bold to raise you; otherwise, your medicine will turn to further sickness."

He helped Meleander to sit up straight.

"Medicine, you bear-doctor?" Meleander asked.

"Yes, medicine," Corax said. "You are mad."

"Trollio! Cleophila!" Meleander called.

"Sir, I am here," Rhetias said.

"I know you, Rhetias," Meleander said. "Please rid the room of this tormenting noise."

He was referring to Corax.

He continued, "He tells me, sirrah, I have taken medicine, Rhetias — medicine, medicine!"

"Sir, it is true, you have," Rhetias said, "and this most learned scholar applied it to you. Oh, you were in a dangerous plight before he took you in hand."

"These things are drunk, plainly drunk," Meleander said.

He was saying that Corax and Rhetias were drunk.

He then asked, "Where did you get your liquor?"

Corax said, "I have never seen a body in the wane of age so overspread with several sorts of such diseases as would make strong youths groan and sink under them."

"All the more is your glory in the miraculous cure," Rhetias said.

Corax said to Rhetias, "Bring in the cordial that was prepared for him to take after his sleep."

The cordial is the good news that will be told to Meleander by various speakers who come from Prince Palador.

Corax said, "It will do Meleander good at heart."

"I hope it will, sir," Rhetias said as he exited.

Meleander said to Corax, "Who do you think I am that you fiddle and play so much upon my patience? Fool, the weight of my disease sits on my heart so heavy that all the hands of skill cannot remove one grain to ease my grief.

"If you could poison my memory, or wrap my senses up into a dullness as hard and cold as flints and if you could make me walk, speak, eat, and laugh without a sense or knowledge of my faculties, why, then, perhaps, at fairs you might make a profit from such a grotesque puppet show and get credit from credulous gazers, but you still would not profit me.

"Study to gull the wise; I am too simple — poor in condition — to be wrought on."

"I'll burn my books, old man," Corax said, "but I will do you good, and quickly, too."

Aretus entered the room; he was carrying letters patent that granted official offices.

Aretus said, "Most honored Lord Meleander, our great master, Prince Palador of Cyprus, has by me sent you these letters patent, in which are contained not only confirmation of the honors you formerly enjoyed, but the additional honor of being the Marshal of Cyprus."

He gave Meleander the letters patent and said, "You have now regained all of your previous honors and gained a new, important honor as well.

"Before long, Prince Palador intends to visit you.

"Excuse my haste: I must leave and wait upon the prince."

Aretus exited.

"There's one pill that works," Corax said.

"Do you know that spirit?" Meleander said. "It is a grave familiar, and talked I know not what."

A familiar is a witch's attendant spirit. Meleander could not believe what was happening.

Corax said, "He's like, I think, the prince's tutor: Aretus."

"Yes, yes," Meleander said. "It may be. I have seen such a formality; it does not matter where or when."

Amethus entered the room, carrying a staff of office.

Amethus said, "Prince Palador has sent you, my lord, this staff of office, and he also salutes you as Grand Commander of the Ports throughout his principalities.

"He shortly will visit you himself. I must leave and wait on him."

He handed Meleander the staff of office and then exited.

Corax asked Meleander, "Do you feel your medicine working yet?"

Meleander replied, "A devil is a rare juggler — trickster — and can cheat the eye, but the devil cannot corrupt the reason that is in the throne of a pure soul."

He still could not believe what was happening.

Sophronos entered the room, carrying a miniature portrait.

"Another familiar spirit!" Meleander said. "I will withstand you. Be and do what you can, I don't care."

Sophronos said, "From Prince Palador, dear brother, I present you this rich relic, a jewel he has long worn in his bosom."

The miniature that he handed to Meleander was a portrait of Eroclea.

"From now on, he told me to say, he does ask you to call him son, for he will call you father. It is an honor, brother, that a subject cannot but entertain with thankful prayers.

Soon, Prince Palador and Meleander would be son-in-law and father-in-law.

Sophronos said, "Be moderate in your joy.

"Prince Palador will be here in person to confirm my errand, but for now he commands my service."

Corax asked Meleander, "What hope do you have now of being cured?"

"Wait! Wait!" Meleander said. "What earthquakes roll in my flesh! Here's prince, and prince, and prince — prince upon prince! The dotage of my sorrows revels in magic of ambitious scorn — I am seeing delusions of things I wish were real.

"Even if these things are enchantments as deadly as the grave, I'll look upon them: letters patent, staff of office, and relic!"

A relic is a memento of a deceased loved person. This relic was the miniature portrait of Eroclea, whom Meleander, her father, thought was dead.

"To the last first," he said as he stood and picked up the miniature portrait and looked at it.

He said, "Surround me, you guarding ministers, and always keep me awake until the cliffs that overhang my sight fall off, and leave these hollow spaces to be crammed with dust!"

He wanted his guardian angels to keep him awake so that he could look at the miniature portrait until he died, his eyelids fell off, and his empty eye sockets filled with dust.

Corax said, "It is time, I see, to fetch the cordial."

The messengers from Prince Palador had been preliminaries to the main medicine, which was Eroclea.

Corax said to Meleander, "Please sit down; I'll quickly be here again."

Meleander said, "Good man, give me leave. I will sit down, indeed. Here's company enough for me to prate to."

Corax exited.

Meleander looked at the miniature portrait and said, "Eroclea! It is the same image as she; the cunning arts-man faltered not in a line. If he could have fashioned a little hollow space here, and blown breath into it and have made it move and whisper, it would have been excellent — but, truly, it is well, it is very well as it is, surpassing, most surpassing well."

Cleophila entered the room, followed by Eroclea and then by Rhetias.

Cleophila said, "The sovereign greatness who, by commission from the powers of heaven, sways both this land and us, our gracious prince, Prince Palador, by me presents you, sir, with this large bounty, a gift more precious to him than his birthright."

She led Eroclea by the hand to Meleander and said, "Here let your cares come to an end; now set at liberty your long-imprisoned heart, and welcome home the solace of your soul, the solace that has been kept from you too long."

Eroclea knelt before Meleander and asked, "Dear sir, do you know me?"

"Yes, you are my daughter, my eldest blessing," Meleander said. "Know you! Why, Eroclea, I never did forget you in your absence.

"Poor soul, how are you?"

"The best of my well-being consists in yours," Eroclea replied.

Meleander said, "Stand up, Eroclea. May the gods, who hitherto have kept us both alive, preserve you always!

"Cleophila, I thank you and Prince Palador.

"I thank you, too, Eroclea, because you would, in pity of my age, take so much pains to live until I might once more look upon you before I broke my heart.

"Oh, it was a piece of piety and duty unexampled!"

Rhetias thought, *The good man relishes his comforts greatly. The sight turns me into a child.*

He was crying.

Eroclea said, "I don't have the words that can express my joys."

"Nor I," Cleophila said.

"Nor I," Meleander said. "Yet let us gaze on one another freely, and fully satisfy ourselves with our eyes. Let me be plain: If I should speak as much as I should speak, I would talk of a thousand things at once, and all of them would be of you, of you, my child, of you!

"My tears, like ruffling winds locked up in caves, bustle to find a vent —"

Aeolus, god of the winds, kept them locked up in a cave and released only the winds he wished to be free for a while. Sometimes he released the violent winds of dark storms, and sometimes he released the calm winds of a sunny summer day.

Meleander continued, "— on the other side: To fly out into mirth would not be so comely."

He had not yet stopped crying.

He said to Eroclea, "Come here; let me kiss you.

"With a pride, strength, courage, and fresh blood, which now your presence has stored me with, I kneel before their altars, whose sovereignty kept guard about your safety.

"Ask, ask your sister, please; she will tell you that I have been much mad."

Cleophila said to Eroclea, "He has been much discontented, shunning all means that might procure comfort for him."

"Heaven has at last been gracious," Eroclea said.

"So say I," Meleander said. "But wherefore drop your words with such sloth, as if you were afraid to mingle truth with your misfortunes? You seem to be afraid to tell me the truth about your misfortunes.

"Understand me thoroughly. I would not have you report fully, from point to point, a journal of your absence — it would take up too much time.

"I would securely use the little remnant of my life listening to you if you might every day be telling some of what you have undergone, which might convey me to my rest with comfort.

"Let me think. How we first parted puzzles my faint remembrance — but soft Cleophila, you told me that Prince Palador sent me this present."

"From his own fair hands, I did receive my sister," Cleophila said.

"To requite him, we will not dig his father's grave anew, although the mention of his father much concerns the business we inquire of," Meleander said.

As a form of repayment to Prince Palador, he would not talk about the prince's father, although he was the reason why Eroclea had disappeared from the court and from Cyprus.

Meleander continued, "As I said, we parted in a hurry at the court. I went to this castle, which afterward became my jail."

He then asked Eroclea, "But where did you go, dear heart?"

Rhetias thought, *Now they fall to it; I looked for this to happen.*

This meeting was something he had long looked forward to witnessing.

Eroclea replied, "I, by my uncle's care, Sophronos, my good uncle, quickly was disguised as a sailor's boy and conveyed on board a ship that very night."

"An acute and strange and cunning trick," Meleander said.

"The ship was bound for Corinth," Eroclea said. "I arrived there first, attended only by your servant Rhetias and all suitable necessaries. From thence, with me wearing the clothing of a youth, we journeyed to Athens, where, until our recent return, we lived safely."

Meleander said, "Oh, what a thing is man to make a league of factions of distempered passions against the sacred Providence above him! Here, in the story of your two years' exile, rare pity and delight are sweetly mixed."

He then asked Eroclea, "And were you still disguised as a boy?"

"Yes — I obeyed my uncle's wise command," Eroclea answered.

"His plot was safely carried out," Meleander said. "I humbly thank your fate."

Eroclea said, "If earthly treasures are poured in plenty down from heaven on mortals, they rain among those oracles that flow in schools of sacred knowledge; such is Athens, yet Athens was to me only a fair prison.

"The thoughts of you, my sister, country, fortunes, and something of the prince, barred all contents that otherwise might have ravished my senses. For had not Rhetias been always comforting to me, certainly things would have gone worse."

"Speak softly, Eroclea," Meleander said. "That 'something of the prince' bears danger in it."

Prince Palador's father had behaved badly, and Meleander still harbored some worry that Prince Palador might possibly behave badly.

Meleander continued, "Yet you have traveled, wench, for such endowments as might create a wife fit for a prince, had he the world to guide, but let's not talk about that.

"How did you come home?"

Rhetias said, "Sir, with your noble favor, kissing your hand first, I can answer that question."

"Honest, right honest Rhetias!" Meleander said.

Rhetias kissed Meleander's hand, and then he said, "Your grave brother — Sophronos — perceived with what a hopeless love his son, Lord Menaphon, too eagerly pursued Thamasta, cousin to our present prince, Prince Palador, and, to remove the violence of affection, sent him to Athens, where, for twelve months' space, your daughter, who is the young lady I serve, and her cousin, who is Lord Menaphon, enjoyed each other's griefs until we were all called home by his father, the Lord Sophronos."

"Enough, enough," Meleander said. "The world shall henceforth witness my thankfulness to heaven and those people who have been full of pity for me and mine.

"Lend me a looking-glass."

He looked down and said, "What! How have I come to be so courtly, dressed in fresh clothing?"

Rhetias said, "Here's the looking-glass, sir."

He handed a mirror to Meleander.

Meleander looked in the mirror and said, "I'm in the trim, too. My hair and beard have been trimmed.

"Oh, Cleophila, this is the result of the goodness of your care and cunning."

Music played loudly.

Meleander asked, "From where is this music coming?"

"The prince, my lord, is here in person," Rhetias said.

All of them knelt.

Prince Palador, Sophronos, Aretus, Amethus, Menaphon, Corax, Thamasta, and Kala all entered the scene.

Using the royal plural, Prince Palador said, "You shall not kneel to us; all of you rise, I command you."

They stood up.

Prince Palador said to Meleander, "Father, you wrong your age; henceforth my arms" — he embraced Meleander — "and heart shall be your guard: We have overheard all the spoken passages of your united loves.

"Be young again, Meleander; live to number a happy generation of grandchildren, and die old in comforts as in years!

"The offices and honors that I lately conferred on you are not fantastic bounties, but are what you deserve.

"Enjoy them liberally."

"My tears must thank you," Meleander said, "for my tongue cannot."

His tears made it difficult to come up with the right words to sufficiently express what he felt.

Corax said to Meleander, "I have kept my promise, and given you a cordial sure to restore your health."

"Oh, a splendid cordial!" Meleander said.

Prince Palador said to Meleander, "Good man, we both have shared enough of sadness, although your sadness has tasted deeper of the extreme. Let us forget it henceforth.

"Where's the picture I sent you? Keep it; it is a counterfeit, and, in exchange for that, I seize on this" — he took Eroclea by the hand — "the real substance.

"With this other hand I give away, before her father's face, his younger joy, Cleophila, to you, cousin Amethus: Take her, and be to her more than a father, a deserving husband.

"Thus, Meleander, robbed of both your children in a minute, your cares are taken off."

"My brains are dulled," Meleander said. "I am entranced, and know not what you mean.

"Great, gracious sir, alas, why do you mock me? I am a weak old man, so poor and feeble that my hard-to-manage joints can scarcely creep to the grave, where I must seek my rest."

"Eroclea was, you know, contracted to be mine in marriage," Prince Palador said. "Cleophila was contracted to be my cousin's in marriage, by consent of both their hearts.

"Amethus and I both now claim our own.

"It only remains for you to give a blessing to our engagements, for confirmation."

"Sir, it is truth and justice," Rhetias said to Meleander.

"May the gods, who lent you, my daughters, to me, bless your vows!" Meleander said. "Oh, children, children, pay your prayers to Heaven, for Heaven has showed much mercy.

"But, Sophronos, you are my brother — I can say no more — a good, good brother!"

Prince Palador said, "Leave the rest to time.

"Cousin Thamasta, I must give you away in marriage, too. She's your wife, Menaphon.

"Rhetias, for you, and for Corax, I have more than common thanks.

"On to the temple! There all solemn rites shall be performed, and a general feast shall be proclaimed.

"The lover's melancholy has found a cure. Sorrows are changed to bride-songs.

"So thrive they whom Fate in spite of storms has kept alive."

EPILOGUE

To be too confident is as unjust
    In any work as too much to distrust:
    [Those] Who from the laws of study have not swerved
    Know begged applauses never were deserved.
    We must submit to censure: so does he
    Whose hours begot this issue; yet, being free,
    For his part, if he has not pleased you, then
    In this kind he'll not trouble you again.

***

Note: Previously, John Ford had co-authored plays, but *The Lover's Melancholy* is sometimes regarded as the first play he wrote as sole author. In the Epilogue, he is saying that he is free: He has other sources of income and need not write plays to make a living; therefore, he is under no obligation to write another play — and if this play is a failure, he in fact will not write another play. Since he wrote as sole author a total of eight surviving plays, we can assume that *The Lover's Melancholy* pleased the audience.

As he predicted in the Prologue, the audience "cured," aka "protected," *THE LOVER'S MELANCHOLY* by applauding it and making it a success.

APPENDIX A: NOTES

— 2.1 —

In Act 2, Scene 1, Amethus says this:

Shall we [go] to the castle?

Later he says:

Sister, soon

Expect us; this day we range the city.

The question I have is this: To whom is he asking his question?

The answer is either 1) Parthenophill, or 2) his [Amethus'] sister, Thamasta.

The answer depends on part whether "[go] to the castle" and "we will range the city" mean different things or the same thing. (It also depends on what Rhetias' "All three — I'll go, too" means.)

If they mean different things, he may be asking his sister, "Shall we [go] to the castle?" A change in plans (the chance to talk to Cleophila alone) then makes him tell his sister to expect them soon.

If they mean the same thing, he may be asking Parthenophill, "Shall we [go] to the castle?"

In the body of this book, I assumed he was talking to Thamasta; however, if I had assumed that he was talking to Parthenophill, I would have written this:

"Shall we go to the castle?" Amethus asked Parthenophill.

"We will accompany you both and render any needed service," Menaphon said.

"We" referred to Menaphon and Rhetias.

"I will accompany all three of you," Rhetias agreed. "I'll go, too."

He whispered to Amethus, "Listen in your ear, gallant; I'll keep the old madman — Meleander — busy by talking to him, while you gabble to Cleophila, his daughter. My thumb's upon my lips; I'll say not a word about this."

"I need not fear that you will reveal anything you should not, Rhetias," Amethus whispered.

Amethus said out loud, "Sister, expect us soon. Today we will wander the city."

"Well, I shall expect you soon," Thamasta said.

THE WHOLE PLAY

Why, oh, why didn't Sophronos (or Menaphon or Rhetias or Eroclea) tell Meleander and Cleophila early that Eroclea was still alive in Greece? That would have saved much misery.

According to a hint by Rhetias in 2.1, Meleander is the one who caused Eroclea to be spirited away. If that is true, his mental illness could be caused by his fall in status and his disgrace at the court. He, however, does not seem to be aware of Eroclea's whereabouts or her health, which are things that he, I believe, could have been informed of.

According to Eroclea in 4.3, it is her uncle, Sophronos, who knew her whereabouts for the two years she had been missing. Therefore, Sophronos could have informed his brother (Eroclea's father) that she was safe in Athens.

Possibly, Rhetias is aware that Sophronos, Eroclea's uncle, is the one who actually arranged her rescue. If so, in 2.1 he may be lying to or deliberately misleading Prince Palador out of suspicion of him.

To be honest, after Prince Palador's father died, a half-hour of conversation between Prince Palador and Sophronos could have cleared everything up. We aren't told when Prince Palador's father died, but there seems to be no good reason why Eroclea had to return home disguised as a young man.

(In 2.1 Rhetias talks about another situation in which the king dies a year or more earlier, and the young woman returns home after receiving notice of the death — the notice came three months before she returned home.)

Even if the reason was fear that Prince Palador might behave badly, as did his father, in 2.1 Rhetias learns that Prince Palador loves Eroclea. Rhetias could then have easily told him outright that Eroclea was alive and well.

Here is a definition of "Idiot plot" from Wikipedia:

In literary criticism, an idiot plot is "a plot which is kept in motion solely by virtue of the fact that everybody involved is an idiot," and where the story would otherwise be over if this were not the case. It is a narrative where its conflict comes from characters not recognizing, or not being told, key information that would resolve the conflict, often because of plot contrivance. The only thing that prevents the conflict's resolution is the character's [or characters'] constant avoidance or obliviousness of it throughout the plot, even if it was already obvious to the viewer, so the characters are all "idiots" in that they are too obtuse to simply resolve the conflict immediately.

Reviewing Prime *in 2005 critic Roger Ebert said "I can forgive and even embrace an Idiot Plot in its proper place (consider [Fred] Astaire and [Ginger] Rogers in* Top Hat*). But when the characters have depth and their decisions have consequences, I grow restless when their misunderstandings could be ended by words that the screenplay refuses to allow them to utter." Alternate formulations describe only the protagonist as being an idiot.*

Source: "Idiot plot." Wikipedia. Accessed 23 June 2019 <https://en.wikipedia.org/wiki/Idiot_plot>.

Let us note, however, that editor R F. Hill identifies "the play's therapy for melancholic states" in this way: "If they are deeply settled then the process, the play suggests, must be gradual" (2).

Source of R. F. Hill quote: Ford, John. *THE LOVER'S MELANCHOLY.* Ed. R. F. Hill. Manchester University Press, 1985.

In 2.1, Aretus says, "Passions of a violent nature are most easily reclaimed by degrees."

In 5.2, however, Meleander receives lots of good news very quickly that cures his deeply settled melancholy.

***

In 3.2 Menaphon criticizes Parthenophill for being his rival for Thamasta's love, but Menaphon spent time with Parthenophill in Greece and must know that Parthenophill is Eroclea, although in 1.1 Menaphon tells Amethus that Parthenophill would reveal little of his background. (Rhetias was apparently with Eroclea, and Menaphon would certainly recognize Rhetias.) In 5.2, it is confirmed that Eroclea and Menaphon shared each other's griefs. Was Menaphon's supposed jealousy of Parthenophill part of a desire to make Thamasta love Menaphon?

***

Part of the frustration of this play is caused by not knowing who knew what and not knowing when they knew it. For example, when did Corax the physician learn Parthenophill's real identity?

***

One minor inconsistency is that Eroclea was supposed to have spent her exile in Athens, but Menaphon claimed to have met Parthenophill in Thessaly; Parthenophill, of course, was Eroclea in disguise as a young man.

Another minor inconsistency is that Meleander had not had his hair and beard trimmed for almost four years, according to Trollio in 2.2. Eroclea, however, was missing for only two years. Rhetias hints at that in 2.1. Meleander confirms the two years' exile in 5.2.

***

Here are two relevant passages explaining the back story:

2.1: Rhetias tells Prince Palador a story:

"My Lord Meleander falling in status, on whose favor my fortunes relied, I furnished myself for travel," Rhetias said, "and I bent my course to Athens; there a pretty incident, after a while, came to my knowledge."

"My ear is open to you," Prince Palador said. "I am listening."

"A young lady engaged to a noble gentleman, as the lady we last mentioned — Eroclea — and your highness were, being hindered by their jarring parents, stole away from her home, and was conveyed disguised as a ship-boy in a merchant ship from the country where she lived, to Corinth first and afterwards to Athens, where in much solitariness she lived, like a youth, almost two years, courted by all for acquaintance, but friend to none by familiarity."

"Was she wearing the clothing of a man?" Prince Palador asked.

"She lived as a handsome young man until, her sweetheart's father having died a year before or more, she received notice of it within the last three months or less, and with much joy returned home, and, as the report in Athens stated, enjoyed the happiness for which she had been long an exile.

"Now, noble sir, if you did love the Lady Eroclea, why may not such safety and fate direct her as directed the other? It is not impossible."

It was not impossible that the Lady Eroclea could return to Cyprus.

5.2: Eroclea's and Rhetias' explanation to Meleander:

Eroclea replied, "I, by my uncle's care, Sophronos, my good uncle, quickly was disguised as a sailor's boy and conveyed on board a ship that very night."

"An acute and strange and cunning trick," Meleander said.

"The ship was bound for Corinth," Eroclea said. "I arrived there first, attended only by your servant Rhetias and all suitable necessaries. From thence, with me wearing the clothing of a youth, we journeyed to Athens, where, until our recent return, we lived safely."

Meleander said, "Oh, what a thing is man to make a league of factions of distempered passions against the sacred Providence above him! Here, in the story of your two years' exile, rare pity and delight are sweetly mixed."

He then asked Eroclea, "And were you still disguised as a boy?"

"Yes — I obeyed my uncle's wise command," Eroclea answered.

"His plot was safely carried out," Meleander said. "I humbly thank your fate."

Eroclea said, "If earthly treasures are poured in plenty down from heaven on mortals, they rain among those oracles that flow in schools of sacred knowledge; such is Athens, yet Athens was to me only a fair prison.

"The thoughts of you, my sister, country, fortunes, and something of the prince, barred all contents that otherwise might have ravished my senses. For had not Rhetias been always comforting to me, certainly things would have gone worse."

"Speak softly, Eroclea," Meleander said. "That 'something of the prince' bears danger in it."

Prince Palador's father had behaved badly, and Meleander still harbored some worry that Prince Palador might possibly behave badly.

Meleander continued, "Yet you have traveled, wench, for such endowments as might create a wife fit for a prince, had he the world to guide, but let's not talk about that.

"How did you come home?"

Rhetias said, "Sir, with your noble favor, kissing your hand first, I can answer that question."

"Honest, right honest Rhetias!" Meleander said.

Rhetias kissed Meleander's hand, and then he said, "Your grave brother — Sophronos — perceived with what a hopeless love his son, Lord Menaphon, too eagerly pursued Thamasta, cousin to our present prince, Prince Palador, and, to

*remove the violence of affection, sent him to Athens, where, for twelve months'
space, your daughter, who is the young lady I serve, and her cousin, who is Lord
Menaphon, enjoyed each other's griefs until we were all called home by his father,
the Lord Sophronos."*

APPENDIX B: ABOUT THE AUTHOR

It was a dark and stormy night. Suddenly a cry rang out, and on a hot summer night in 1954, Josephine, wife of Carl Bruce, gave birth to a boy — me. Unfortunately, this young married couple allowed Reuben Saturday, Josephine's brother, to name their first-born. Reuben, aka "The Joker," decided that Bruce was a nice name, so he decided to name me Bruce Bruce. I have gone by my middle name — David — ever since.

Being named Bruce David Bruce hasn't been all bad. Bank tellers remember me very quickly, so I don't often have to show an ID. It can be fun in charades, also. When I was a counselor as a teenager at Camp Echoing Hills in Warsaw, Ohio, a fellow counselor gave the signs for "sounds like" and "two words," then she pointed to a bruise on her leg twice. Bruise Bruise? Oh yeah, Bruce Bruce is the answer!

Uncle Reuben, by the way, gave me a haircut when I was in kindergarten. He cut my hair short and shaved a small bald spot on the back of my head. My mother wouldn't let me go to school until the bald spot grew out again.

Of all my brothers and sisters (six in all), I am the only transplant to Athens, Ohio. I was born in Newark, Ohio, and have lived all around Southeastern Ohio. However, I moved to Athens to go to Ohio University and have never left.

At Ohio U, I never could make up my mind whether to major in English or Philosophy, so I got a bachelor's degree with a double major in both areas, then I added a Master of Arts degree in English and a Master of Arts degree in Philosophy. Yes, I have my MAMA degree.

Currently, and for a long time to come (I eat fruits and veggies), I am spending my retirement writing books such as *Nadia Comaneci: Perfect 10*, *The Funniest People in Dance*, *Homer's* Iliad: *A Retelling in Prose*, and *William Shakespeare's* Othello: *A Retelling in Prose*.

By the way, my sister Brenda Kennedy writes romances such as *A New Beginning* and *Shattered Dreams*.

APPENDIX C: SOME BOOKS BY DAVID BRUCE

Retellings of a Classic Work of Literature

Arden of Faversham: *A Retelling*

Ben Jonson's The Alchemist: *A Retelling*

Ben Jonson's The Arraignment, or Poetaster: *A Retelling*

Ben Jonson's Bartholomew Fair: *A Retelling*

Ben Jonson's The Case is Altered: *A Retelling*

Ben Jonson's Catiline's Conspiracy: *A Retelling*

Ben Jonson's The Devil is an Ass: *A Retelling*

Ben Jonson's Epicene: *A Retelling*

Ben Jonson's Every Man in His Humor: *A Retelling*

Ben Jonson's Every Man Out of His Humor: *A Retelling*

Ben Jonson's The Fountain of Self-Love, or Cynthia's Revels: *A Retelling*

Ben Jonson's The Magnetic Lady, or Humors Reconciled: *A Retelling*

Ben Jonson's The New Inn, or The Light Heart: *A Retelling*

Ben Jonson's Sejanus' Fall: *A Retelling*

Ben Jonson's The Staple of News: *A Retelling*

Ben Jonson's A Tale of a Tub: *A Retelling*

Ben Jonson's Volpone, or the Fox: *A Retelling*

Christopher Marlowe's Complete Plays: Retellings

Christopher Marlowe's Dido, Queen of Carthage: *A Retelling*

Christopher Marlowe's Doctor Faustus: *Retellings of the 1604 A-Text and of the 1616 B-Text*

Christopher Marlowe's Edward II: *A Retelling*

Christopher Marlowe's The Massacre at Paris: *A Retelling*

Christopher Marlowe's The Rich Jew of Malta: *A Retelling*

Christopher Marlowe's Tamburlaine, Parts 1 and 2: *Retellings*

Dante's Divine Comedy: *A Retelling in Prose*

Dante's Inferno: *A Retelling in Prose*

Dante's Purgatory: *A Retelling in Prose*

Dante's Paradise: *A Retelling in Prose*

The Famous Victories of Henry V: *A Retelling*

From the Iliad *to the* Odyssey: *A Retelling in Prose of Quintus of Smyrna's* Posthomerica

George Chapman, Ben Jonson, and John Marston's Eastward Ho! *A Retelling*

George Peele's The Arraignment of Paris: *A Retelling*

George Peele's The Battle of Alcazar: *A Retelling*

George Peele's David and Bathsheba, and the Tragedy of Absalom: *A Retelling*

George Peele's Edward I: *A Retelling*

George Peele's The Old Wives' Tale: *A Retelling*

George-a-Greene: *A Retelling*
The History of King Leir: *A Retelling*
Homer's Iliad: *A Retelling in Prose*
Homer's Odyssey: *A Retelling in Prose*
J.W. Gent.'s The Valiant Scot: *A Retelling*
Jason and the Argonauts: A Retelling in Prose of Apollonius of Rhodes' Argonautica
John Ford: Eight Plays Translated into Modern English
John Ford's The Broken Heart: *A Retelling*
John Ford's The Fancies, Chaste and Noble: *A Retelling*
John Ford's The Lady's Trial: *A Retelling*
John Ford's The Lover's Melancholy: *A Retelling*
John Ford's Love's Sacrifice: *A Retelling*
John Ford's Perkin Warbeck: *A Retelling*
John Ford's The Queen: *A Retelling*
John Ford's 'Tis Pity She's a Whore: *A Retelling*
John Lyly's Campaspe: *A Retelling*
John Lyly's Endymion, The Man in the Moon: *A Retelling*
John Lyly's Galatea: *A Retelling*
John Lyly's Love's Metamorphosis: *A Retelling*
John Lyly's Midas: *A Retelling*
John Lyly's Mother Bombie: *A Retelling*
John Lyly's Sappho and Phao: *A Retelling*
John Lyly's The Woman in the Moon: *A Retelling*
John Webster's The White Devil: *A Retelling*
King Edward III: *A Retelling*
Mankind: *A Medieval Morality Play* (A Retelling)
Margaret Cavendish's The Unnatural Tragedy: *A Retelling*
The Merry Devil of Edmonton: *A Retelling*
The Summoning of Everyman: *A Medieval Morality Play* (A Retelling)
Robert Greene's Friar Bacon and Friar Bungay: *A Retelling*
The Taming of a Shrew: *A Retelling*
Tarlton's Jests: A Retelling
Thomas Middleton's A Chaste Maid in Cheapside: *A Retelling*
Thomas Middleton's Women Beware Women: *A Retelling*
Thomas Middleton and Thomas Dekker's The Roaring Girl: *A Retelling*
Thomas Middleton and William Rowley's The Changeling: *A Retelling*
The Trojan War and Its Aftermath: Four Ancient Epic Poems
Virgil's Aeneid: *A Retelling in Prose*
William Shakespeare's 5 Late Romances: Retellings in Prose
William Shakespeare's 10 Histories: Retellings in Prose
William Shakespeare's 11 Tragedies: Retellings in Prose
William Shakespeare's 12 Comedies: Retellings in Prose

William Shakespeare's 38 Plays: Retellings in Prose
William Shakespeare's 1 Henry IV, aka Henry IV, Part 1: *A Retelling in Prose*
William Shakespeare's 2 Henry IV, aka Henry IV, Part 2: *A Retelling in Prose*
William Shakespeare's 1 Henry VI, aka Henry VI, Part 1: *A Retelling in Prose*
William Shakespeare's 2 Henry VI, aka Henry VI, Part 2: *A Retelling in Prose*
William Shakespeare's 3 Henry VI, aka Henry VI, Part 3: *A Retelling in Prose*
William Shakespeare's All's Well that Ends Well: *A Retelling in Prose*
William Shakespeare's Antony and Cleopatra: *A Retelling in Prose*
William Shakespeare's As You Like It: *A Retelling in Prose*
William Shakespeare's The Comedy of Errors: *A Retelling in Prose*
William Shakespeare's Coriolanus: *A Retelling in Prose*
William Shakespeare's Cymbeline: *A Retelling in Prose*
William Shakespeare's Hamlet: *A Retelling in Prose*
William Shakespeare's Henry V: *A Retelling in Prose*
William Shakespeare's Henry VIII: *A Retelling in Prose*
William Shakespeare's Julius Caesar: *A Retelling in Prose*
William Shakespeare's King John: *A Retelling in Prose*
William Shakespeare's King Lear: *A Retelling in Prose*
William Shakespeare's Love's Labor's Lost: *A Retelling in Prose*
William Shakespeare's Macbeth: *A Retelling in Prose*
William Shakespeare's Measure for Measure: *A Retelling in Prose*
William Shakespeare's The Merchant of Venice: *A Retelling in Prose*
William Shakespeare's The Merry Wives of Windsor: *A Retelling in Prose*
William Shakespeare's A Midsummer Night's Dream: *A Retelling in Prose*
William Shakespeare's Much Ado About Nothing: *A Retelling in Prose*
William Shakespeare's Othello: *A Retelling in Prose*
William Shakespeare's Pericles, Prince of Tyre: *A Retelling in Prose*
William Shakespeare's Richard II: *A Retelling in Prose*
William Shakespeare's Richard III: *A Retelling in Prose*
William Shakespeare's Romeo and Juliet: *A Retelling in Prose*
William Shakespeare's The Taming of the Shrew: *A Retelling in Prose*
William Shakespeare's The Tempest: *A Retelling in Prose*
William Shakespeare's Timon of Athens: *A Retelling in Prose*
William Shakespeare's Titus Andronicus: *A Retelling in Prose*
William Shakespeare's Troilus and Cressida: *A Retelling in Prose*
William Shakespeare's Twelfth Night: *A Retelling in Prose*
William Shakespeare's The Two Gentlemen of Verona: *A Retelling in Prose*
William Shakespeare's The Two Noble Kinsmen: *A Retelling in Prose*
William Shakespeare's The Winter's Tale: *A Retelling in Prose*